the *Samurai*
and the **Mujahideen**

the *Samurai*
and the **Mujahideen**

Ben Dowling

Sirena Press
Madeira Beach, Fl

Sirena Press
An imprint of Murmaid Publishing

For information:
Murmaid Publishing
PO Box 86592
Madeira Beach, FL 33738
theMurmaid@tampabay.rr.com

ISBN 978-0-9819432-2-0

Cover and Book Design
theMurmaid ™

First English edition

Printed in the United States of America

To order additional copies: theMurmaid@TampaBay.rr.com

Prologue

I think this story came to me, the beginnings of the story anyway—from my high school years, when I read *Soldier of Fortune Magazine.*

Their coverage of the Soviet war in Afghanistan has stuck with me for twenty plus years.

Eight years ago I began reading about Afghanistan again. *Soldiers of God* by Robert Kaplan, and *Ghost Wars* by Steve Coll, *Sacred Rage* by Robin Wright sticks out, more a synopsis of the Islamic terrorism wave. There is a chapter on Osama bin Laden during the Soviet Afghan war.

So, my story begins:

It's late fall–1983, almost four years after the Red Army's invasion of Afghanistan, and the Islamic warriors, known as the mujahideen, continue their bloody struggle against the superior military power of the Soviet Union.

Two complete strangers, Jack Randall a US Rangers-Vietnam veteran turned smuggler, and Toshi Ushido, a highly trained Japanese martial artist turned commodities broker, are sent by a wealthy Chinese entrepreneur with anti-communist sympathies to "assist" the same mujahideen group. They form an unintended alliance.

The story begins in Peshawar, Pakistan where the two meet, and accompany a Pashtun militia leader to a village in the Nangarhar province of southeastern Afghanistan. Toshi goes north to Jalalabad to fight alongside the group, as Jack goes west to Kabul to give a demonstration of the strategic value of a well placed sniper.

1

During the last week of October, 1983, I flew from Kowloon, Hong Kong to New Delhi, India and boarded the train for a three thousand kilometer ride through Lahore, Pakistan and to the Peshawar Station.

Stepping down onto the platform, I saw a big round thermometer hanging over the station entrance, the single clock hand pointed to twenty-degrees. I quickly did the Celsius to Fahrenheit conversion in my head, it was about seventy.

"Welcome to the City of Flowers," said the Indian conductor with his nasally-musical accent.

There were no flowers, just a whole lot of people, and a bad smell.

With directions to the Cantonment district of New Peshawar, I found the Dean's Hotel, a big two-story Victorian, made of baked-brick with a whitewashed look. Inside, polished hardwood floors, embossed floor-to-ceiling mirrors, and ornate silver-chandeliers greeted me.

"Excuse me," said the desk-clerk with an unmistakably British accent, "but it says here that there are two people in your party."

I couldn't tell if he was being snotty or not. I signed the registration, and walked away.

"Nope, just me."

My suite was huge, bigger than I was used to, with a big bathroom, two double-beds, and a sitting room complete with a brick fireplace.

While washing off the dust and smell of the train in a long hot shower, I thought about turning thirty-three in less than two months, and what little I'd done with my life so far. I was out of money, and out of ideas, when Pik Hsun, a Chinese quasi-mafioso and my old boss called me from Hong Kong.

"I have a job for you," he said, "why don't you come back to Kowloon. I'll tell you all about the job then. Get a cab to the airport, there will be a first-class ticket to Katak International waiting for you, I'll pick you up. OK?"

I didn't have anything better to do.

"See you in a few," I replied.

"One more thing," he said, "what are you looking like these days? Still wearing your hair high and tight, and clean-shaven like when you got out of the Army in '71?"

"No," I said. "Right now I have long shaggy hair and a bushy beard. But I'll see a barber before I get on the plane."

"No don't shave the beard or cut your hair," said Pik, "it'll make it easier for you to blend in."

I dried-off, put on a clean shirt, and ordered a plate of boiled chicken and potatoes, with a loaf of fresh-baked bread and a pot of tea. I'm not a tea drinker, but thought I should get away from drinking beer all of the time. I ate and napped for a while, before going to find the Saddar-Road Teahouse for a meeting with an Afghan tribesman named Mahmoud Shinwari.

I found the Teahouse easily. Inside was a big, rough-looking crowd. The place was a meeting point near the border for fighters going into Afghanistan. There brothers-in-arms planned their next attack, or found their next guns-for-hire job. Pik had told me that these guys were real hard-core Muslims called mujahideen, and that meant they were soldiers of God, and didn't drink any alcohol, but I guess the Non-Muslim mercenaries that they were here to re-cruit did. The teahouse sold bottles of beer, out of an ice-chest.

The Afghan freedom fighters didn't really have a lot of money to offer the Guns who showed up, but it was like free on-the-job-training for aspiring guerrillas, good for résumé-building or free thera-py for those with scores to settle.

Between the few words of Urdu an old man on the train taught me, and the broken English the

Paki waiter spoke, I was able to get a beer and a working description of Mahmoud: medium-height, medium-build, with a thick-gray-beard, wearing a dark green turban and a black shalwar kameez. I sat down at a table in the center of the room.

Unfortunately that description matched about seventy percent of the people there. Pik was right, I don't look all that different than these guys. but after a few minutes I noticed a man in a green turban looking at me. I was pretty-sure it was him, sitting in the far corner, on the floor, surrounded by a few other men with black beards and turbans. I thought I'd finish my beer and go over and introduce myself.

I noticed a Japanese guy sitting by himself at the end of the bar, quietly drinking water and eating bar nuts, so I wondered over. He spoke English so we talked for a while: he was from Tokyo and was also there to see Mahmoud.

It looked to me like Mahmoud was about to leave, so I went over to introduce us. But just as I put my hand out and opened my mouth.

"You are Jack Randall," he said, "Army Rangers, Vietnam Veteran."

"Yes I am..."

"I spoke to your employer, Pik Hsun, in Hong Kong, a few days ago; he said you would be here to-night. He also mentioned that you would have five hundred thousand dollars American, an initial payment."

I just nodded, didn't really want to whip it out

right there.

"And you are Toshi Ushido from Tokyo," Mahmoud continued, "he said you would also be here tonight."

The fact that Pik hadn't mentioned Toshi before startled me a little, but it wasn't the first time he'd withheld information.

"Your cargo will arrive tomorrow on the Lahore mail-train, but now, have you something to show me?"

"Yes," said Toshi.

Mahmoud stepped aside to let two of the other turbaned-men come forward. Then three Asians, beardless with shaved heads, joined with the others crowding in on Toshi. I know I'd only just met him, but I couldn't let him fight five guys by himself, so I stepped up.

Mahmoud caught my eye, and his expression told me to back-off.

"No Jack," said Toshi, "this is my test."

I sat down, I remember thinking that he kind of looked like a Japanese Bruce Lee, same build, maybe a little shorter, but I couldn't see that he was the least bit nervous. Looked like he'd just popped a Quaalude.

The five of them circled Toshi. He was facing the Afghans; the Asian Muslims were behind him. The two Afghans were bigger than him, and the larger of the two stepped up first.

He wound up and threw a right, but Toshi blocked it easily; then he threw a left, and he blocked that one too. The Asians were all about the same size as Toshi. And as he was dodging the frontal assault from the Afghan, the middle Asian rushed him from behind.

With only a glance, Toshi did a high spinning back kick that landed in the center of his attacker's forehead and the guy went down. He was finished.

Toshi still looked completely relaxed, circling around, eyeballing all four of them and then stopped in front of the Afghans. They both charged him, and he dove to his left, tucking into a tight roll.

When both Afghans stopped their charge and turned to face him, he launched straight-up, firing a left-footed roundhouse kick that connected with the first guy's right temple, slamming him onto a table which crashed to the floor, and he followed with a straight leg-stomp to the solar plexus of the other guy, who went straight over on his back with his arms outstretched. Just like in the Nestea ad without a swimming pool. They were both finished.

The two remaining Asian Muslims looked as if they might be trained in the fighting arts, and they coordinated a final assault. They were separated by about two meters, and Toshi was in the middle, in front of them. The one on the right exploded with an all-out kicking attack, left, right, left, right, left; all that Toshi could do was back up and block.

While the kicking assault was driving him back to the wall, the other guy came flying over the kicker's head with his left leg out straight in a blade-kick.

At the last-minute, Toshi side-stepped it, and spun around to deliver a backward right-leg donkey-kick to his chest; throwing him out of the fight. He spun around again to come in below a right round-house kick to sweep the left leg out from under the last man standing, putting him down on his back, bouncing his head off the ground. Then to keep the guy from getting-up again, Toshi brought his elbow down on the bridge of his opponent's nose. Lights-out.

Afterwards, the five slowly got up and walked over to where Mahmoud was sitting. Mahmoud came forward smiling, with his hand extended to Toshi, who wasn't even breathing heavy. They shook hands and Mahmoud introduced himself.

I was still wrapping my head around the idea that Pik had purposely not told me about Toshi. The mystery of the giant hotel room and why the clerk thought there would be two checking-in became clear to me.

2

Back at the hotel, I pulled the mattress from one of the double beds and carried it out to the living room where I threw it on the floor in front of the fireplace. Before going to sleep, I took another shower.

"Once you get to Dean's," Pik said when he dropped me at Kai Tak, "order room service, sleep in, and take a few long, hot showers. When you leave Peshawar, you'll be roughing it for about eight months; crapping in an outhouse, no running-water, and up in the morning with the Chanticleer."

What the fuck is a Chanticleer?

In the shower, I wondered why Pik hadn't told me about Toshi. I wasn't too worried about it though, just didn't like being left in the dark. Afterwards, I built a fire and watched it burn down some before falling asleep.

The next morning, I slept till about eight o'clock, got up and did my morning exercises, two hundred push-ups and two hundred sit-ups, and then Toshi and I went down for breakfast.

We sat under an umbrella on the hotel's manicured lawn.

"Two crescents and tea," I gave the waiter my order.

I was taking in the view of big mountains in the distance, to the west and northwest.

"Those are the Hindu Kush Mountains," said the waiter.

Toshi ordered tea, and said something about picking up his cargo shipment from New Delhi.

"Yeah, wasn't Mahmoud talking about that last night?" and without waiting for an answer, added, "What's in it?"

He told me about making a deal with Mahmoud to supply the mujahideen with three new Toyota four-wheel-drive pickup trucks, $10,000 in small-arms, and medical supplies, for a place to stay, food to eat, and the opportunity to prove himself "on the field of battle."

After watching him kick the shit out of those five guys at the teahouse, I was pretty-sure he was serious, even though he didn't really look the part; he looked like an accountant.

"Up until a little over a year ago," he said, "I was a commodities broker on the Tokyo Stock Exchange. I worked at the Bank of Tokyo advising the bank's customers."

Thought so...

"That's where I met Pik Hsun; he was looking to invest several million dollars in the Exchange—"

I stopped him.

"We'll come back to Pik, but first I want to know where you learned to fight like that!"

"My father taught me Martial Arts, starting when I was five-years-old with karate, the art of empty-handed fighting. Every couple of years after that, he introduced another fighting-art for me to study.

"After karate came kendo, the way of the sword, or Japanese Fencing. It's practiced in pairs, using bokken, wooden swords, and heavy pads. Next I studied kyudo," he sipped his tea, "the way of the bow, or Japanese Archery.

"For a longtime, all I did was practice drawing the bow, without ever firing an arrow. My father pushed me very hard, but it was okay because I wanted to be something in his eyes. My best friend and sparring partner, Yaguda, and I trained for many years, and then we began competing against others and soon we were undefeated.

"On my seventeenth birthday, my father presented me with an old steel katana, Japanese sword, which had been in our family for more than three centuries. Over the next few years I studied additional sword techniques, and began spending most of my time training alone. I forgot about everything and everyone else, but then after sixteen years I stopped practicing martial arts completely."

"How come you quit?"

"Well, when I was twenty-one my mother contracted leukemia and died a month later. Losing her destroyed my father. I felt guilty about it for a while."

"Yeah, my mom died when I was eleven," I interrupted, "on my birthday no less, and it was five years before I found out. I spent five years wondering why she never tried to get in touch with me. Fuuuuuck ... oh, I'm sorry, please continue."

"Anyway, for a while I turned to Buddhism. Countless hours of drilling on the kata became countless hours of meditating on the koan."

"What's a koan?" I asked.

"I'm sure there are a million answers to that question," he said, "but I'll give you this one, a koan is a word puzzle that's not necessarily supposed to be solved, but only to be pondered."

"Huh?"

"It is a point on which to focus your mind's attention while meditating. It's very difficult to clear your mind of all thoughts, but the koan can replace them, the jumble of troubling ideas, giving you just one thing to think about."

I'm not going to say that I was perfectly clear on it, but I was beginning to understand.

"Here's just an example," he said. "Living in Hong Kong for so long, I'm sure you've probably heard this one, at least in passing: 'Two hands clap and there is a sound, but what is the sound of one hand clapping?' And this is one that I came up with myself: 'A fish swims through an ocean of water, but what swims through an ocean of sand?'"

"Anyway...," I realized that I had interrupted him again, and asked him to continue, promising I wouldn't do it again.

"After four years of searching for an answer to the question: why did she have to die, my father, who had become a Buddhist himself, convinced me that I would not find an answer, 'meditation will only lead to acceptance, not understanding'."

"The Tokyo Stock Exchange huh?" I said, interrupting again to change the subject, "bet you had to have a lot of schooling for that."

"Yes, at twenty-five I went to the University of Tokyo where I received undergraduate degrees in mathematics and physics; then I continued on to grad school for a Ph.D. in mathematics, focusing on statistical theory and stochastic processes. It took almost ten years, but when I graduated in 1979, I was quickly hired by the Bank of Tokyo. That was four years ago."

We only had about twenty minutes before Mahmoud was supposed to meet us out front.

"Last question, what was that about proving yourself on the battlefield?"

He glanced at his watch.

"I don't think we have time for me to go into it right now," he said, "until later let me just say, last year my father told me, on his deathbed, that the only way a person can ever really know himself is by facing Death."

What the fuck?

Mahmoud showed up with four black-bearded, turbaned men at half past ten, none were the fighters from the night before.

We walked through a crowded open market-place to the train station.

3

I hadn't seen so many people, in one place, since I was in Kowloon in the mid-seventies. The odors of exotic spices, sweat, shit, gunpowder and hashish were overwhelming, and the noise of the mob was deafening.

"These are the war refugees of Afghanistan," Mahmoud gestured. "You should see the camps, compared to them, this is nothing."

We were at the depot by ten-fifty, the train still hadn't arrived at quarter past eleven. A few minutes before noon, a loudspeaker came on saying something, I have no idea what. Immediately afterwards, Mahmoud and the four men excused themselves.

"It's time for Salaat," he said.

Whatever that means.

The Mail-Train finally came in a half hour later, just as Mahmoud and the others got back.

The three arriving 4x4 pick-ups were brown

with no air-conditioning or radio; spare tires were in the backs of each. Two separate shipping containers holding medical and food supplies, as well as some camping equipment and Toshi's personal martial weapons, came in too.

We emptied the containers, packing the items into the back of two trucks, and covered the beds with tarpaulins.

The guns were to be picked up in a small village south of Peshawar. Because the roads were so congested, we left the two supply-loaded trucks behind, to be guarded by another group that included the Afghans from the teahouse.

Toshi, Mahmoud, a guy named Mazar, and I took the third truck. Toshi and Mazar rode in back while Mahmoud drove forty or so kilometers through the dry, mountainous Kohat Frontier to Darra Adam Khel, a small shanty town with one main road and no power lines.

Mahmoud explained that the expert gunsmiths worked efficiently on electric lathes and drill presses powered by gasoline generators.

"They can make perfect copies of anything from Soviet Kalashnikov AK-47s to NSV DShK 12.7 mm heavy machine-guns."

The shop foreman, Abdullah, was just finishing a kalakov, the name given to the AK-47 by Afghan insurgents. Out of curiosity I inspected it, and compared it to Mahmoud's original, and besides the fact that Mahmoud's gun had fired several thousand rounds, there was no difference between the two. He had gone so far as to copy the serial numbers from the original onto the counterfeit.

I flashed on the Type 56/SKS, the Chinese copy of the AK-47. When I was in Vietnam, I never trusted the M-16. I liked M-14s, but they had been phased out of combat use by 1970, and used only for training after that. I suppose 16s were fairly accurate, but didn't have the knock-down stopping power of the M-14s, they just shredded fuckers. The M-16 would sure put a lot of lead in the air, but I heard a few stories about GIs getting killed in firefights while trying to clear jams – piece of shit. The SKS, on the other hand, was about the most reliable assault rifle I've ever seen, whatever the conditions.

Hell, I once ran one of those communist guns through a ditch, soaking the action with mud, and it still fired when I squeezed the trigger. The first month I was in the shit, I took an SKS, with the folding spike bayonet from one of my former opponents, and was going to use that instead of my M-16, but Sergeant Honcho caught me, and he chewed me real good.

"You stupid motherfucker! When you start shooting that fuckin' thing, you're gonna draw American fire!"

I deserved the dress-down, I wasn't thinking straight; the sound of an AK-47 is pretty distinct.

But soon after that, I started using a 12-gauge-pump. Yeah I know, shotguns are kinda slow to reload, but on patrol I always ran either point or drag—first or last, and my 870 never let me down. When you're panicked, and you have a rifle, you can't always hit a guy coming out of the bush at fifty meters on the first shot, but with a scattergun, it's hard to miss.

Anyway, we got about fifty AK-47 and twelve NSV DShK copies with 1,000 rounds for each; the Soviets called the NSV heavy machine gun a dushka, which is Russian for sweetie. An added bonus to using the same weapons as the Red Army, was that there would never be a shortage of ammo. We loaded the guns into the truck, and Toshi gave Abdullah $10,000 American. Abdullah threw-in four captured RPG-7s and twelve rocket grenades.

After the deal, Mahmoud and Abdullah went to the Mosque. Upon their return, Abdullah's son served us a large meal of boiled goat and wild rice with tea and apricots.

It took us about forty five minutes to get back to Peshawar, arriving about five o'clock.

"We will wait here until after sunset before crossing the border," Mahmoud said, "the darker it is the better. Hinds do not usually fly when it gets dark."

The Mi-24 Hind attack helicopter was quite a problem.

The same loudspeaker went off again, Toshi said something about the muezzin and the adhan.

"We must give Salaat now, be back soon," said Mahmoud.

He and the others grabbed their prayer rugs and

left for the Mosque. I don't have anything against someone wanting to be religious, but thought that maybe I should know how often they would do this Salaat thing. Mahmoud must've seen my concern.

"We pray five, sometimes six times a day. And you should never interrupt the Salaat," he said.

They came back an hour later, as the sun was setting. The sky was that deep orange-red you only see in the Fall.

"We should get ready to go," said Mahmoud, "this is Jafir and Hassan, they will bring up the rear, this is Khaleed, he and I will lead. You and Toshi will follow me, Mazar will ride with you, he knows the way and speaks English too."

I was driving when we left Peshawar, Toshi sat by the rolled-down window, and Mazar was between us.

"Our destination is Sra Kala," said Mazar, "a small village in the Achin district of Nangarhar province, Eastern Afghanistan, from here we go west fifteen kilometers to Jamrud, and follow the road west-northwest to the village of Shadi Bargiar."

Forty minutes later, he pointed out two small streams that over time formed a huge gorge.

"This has been known throughout history as the Gateway to Central Asia. From Darius the Great of Persia, in the fifth century BC, to Alexander the Great, two centuries later, to the Mughals, in the sixteenth century AD, to the British, three centuries later, Many armies have witnessed the treachery of the famous Khyber Pass."

It was too dark to see much, we had blacked out the headlights with visqueen and duct tape earlier. I tried to imagine being under attack from mountain guerrillas, while Mazar continued tour-guiding for us.

"These are the Safed Kuh mountains. This road twists fifty-five kilometers through the Pass, it starts at approximately five hundred meters elevation, and climbs to just over one thousand meters in about twenty-two kilometers to the former British out-post, Fort Ali Masjid."

The walls of the Pass closed in to less than a hundred meters.

"Shortly we'll reach Landi Kotal, a small fort, village and market-place. At more than one thou-sand two hundred meters, it is the highest point of the Khyber Pass. This Fort was once garrisoned by the legendary Khyber Rifles, a unit of the Frontier Corps established in the 1880s and soldiered by Afridis tribesmen from the North West Frontier Province of Pakistan. They were led by command-ers from the British Indian Army's Indian regi-ments."

I could feel a definite descent now.

"We are coming to Landi Khana, a Pashtun village in the Shinwari territory. We will enter Af-ghanistan at the village of Towr Kham, and con-tinue down the valley to the abandoned Afghan Fort of Haft Cha and opening on the Lowyah Dakkah Plain. Once through the Pass, we will contin-ue west another forty kilometers, most of the road is good, but some is soft, and will require care. Just follow Mahmoud. Wake me if there's a helicopter," Mazar said, and put his head down.

We arrived at the village after midnight. Mah-moud showed me and Toshi to a small two-room house.

"These are your quarters; I will see you in the morning..."

Not expecting them to have guest-quarters for me, I'd brought a tent and sleeping bag with me, but this little house, with beds and a fireplace, was a pleasant surprise.

After he left, Toshi unpacked the footlocker that contained his weapons; swords, knives, bows and arrows.

"You don't like guns much do you?" I asked.

Actually, I have a few."

Out of the duffel bag he'd been carrying since we met in Peshawar, he pulled-out an IMI Galil assault rifle with a folding-stock, and a .45 long-slide bowling-pin gun.

"I joined the bank's shooting team when I first started working there, and since then I have col-lected these." He cycled the action on each weapon before he passed them to me.

"Very nice," I said.

"I'm a pretty good shot too," he smiled, "but I prefer the bow and the sword."

4

The next morning, Mahmoud gave us a quick tour of the village. There were two rows of small two or three room plywood shacks lining an unpaved road, just like a frontier town in the old west.

At one end of the road were two barns and a mud brick house surrounded by a two meter wall.

"That is where the chieftain of Sra Kala lives," he pointed out.

At the other end was a M.A.S.H hospital tent, parked out front was the truck loaded with medical supplies.

Mahmoud introduced Toshi and me to an older man named Hamid.

"Toshi has brought many lifesaving medicines," he said to the man.

While Hamid and Toshi unloaded the truck, Mahmoud and I entered the tent. Inside were a handful of beds filled with critically wounded men, it was terribly unsanitary.

"Infection is rampant and often unpreventable," he said.

I'm sure that just simple Clorox or Listerine would be a wonder drug here.

"The weather contributes to the conditions. Afghanistan has what they call a Continental Climate. In the summer, it is very hot, and the winters are very cold with a lot of snow," he explained.

We came to the last bed in the line of wounded men.

"The number of wounded isn't as high as I expected," I said.

"Most of the wounded do not live long enough to get here," he replied sourly, "besides these are only the men…"

I pushed through a curtain into another room; it was full of children.

There were twice as many children as men.

"Children are often the worst casualties of war, either directly or indirectly. These," he gestured, "are some of the direct casualties of this war."

The children, ten years old and younger, were certainly not combatants, but they had been targeted as such. The injuries were not fatal, but they were horrible and often crippling. Feet, legs, hands, and sometimes an entire arm had been blown off. We stopped at the foot of a bed where a young boy, wearing a bandage on his face and missing his right hand, lie sleeping.

"This boy here," he said, "lost both of his parents in a Soviet rocket attack two years ago. That was before I arrived."

The boy started to stir, but Mahmoud kept talking.

"After that, his paternal grandmother took care of him as best she could, but not having a father figure to warn him of the dangers that surround us led to his injury, he lost his hand and part of his nose."

His eyes were open now. I thought he might be startled to wake-up with a stranger staring down at him, but I don't think he was.

"He may be small and handicapped," Mahmoud smiled at the injured boy, "but I assure you, Zmarak here, is quite fierce."

He bared his teeth at the boy, who in turn put on his own war-face. He smiled again and patted the boy's head.

We walked over to a desk where Mahmoud opened the top drawer to show me an antipersonnel mine.

"This has been defused," he said, "so that we may use it to show the children, and warn them not to pick it up."

I'd seen mines like it before; the Army used them in Vietnam. This was the Soviet version of the dragon-tooth APM.

About the size of a 3 x 5 card, tan in color, made of soft-plastic, and filled with a liquid explosive. The mines are wing-shaped to make them aerodynamic so they can be air-dropped. They look like toys.

The little mines can be laid by a plane or helicopter equipped with a mine-dispenser and routing chute. But usually a helicopter is used because they are more maneuverable at lower altitudes. The helicopter deploying these mines flies about twenty meters above the ground, so the mines can be placed with ninety percent accuracy. A mine-laying helicopter can deploy one mine per second for as long as there is a soldier present to reload the dispenser.

The dispenser is portable, about the size of a large suitcase, electronically activated, and fed by a magazine-container. The container holds four clips, with mines arranged in sixteen-mine clips. The chute is just a gutter, maybe a meter long.

As each mine is ejected through the chute, a small latch removes the safety tabs. Once removed, a spring mechanism surrounded by a viscous gelatin pushes and rotates the plunger until it is in line with the detonator; this usually takes from one to forty-five minutes, depending on the air temperature. Once the process has finished, the mine is armed and cannot be disarmed.

Toshi came over to us after unloading the supplies, and Mahmoud left the tent. Moments later he came back with a black guy and two young Asian women, all wearing surgical scrubs.

Marcus was a doctor from Chicago. He looked to be about the same age as me, maybe a little older. He said he'd been a Corpsman stationed in South Vietnam at Dao Phu Quoc below the Me-kong Delta, from '69 to '71.

"I never made it that far south," I said, "stayed mostly in Quang Nam Province."

"Danang right?" he said.

I nodded.

"Yeah I been there…when I got back stateside, I took the GI Bill all the way through med-school."

"What in the world brought you to Afghanistan? You know its still South Asia?" I joked.

"Yeah, let me just say that I missed the action."

He turned to Toshi.

"The medical supplies that you've brought are a true miracle," he said, "many lives will be saved."

The women, Naghma and Badrai, were from Pakistan. Both were fresh out of the Academie Nationale de Medicine in Paris, where they had been in an Exchange, Out Reach Scholarship program. The three doctors were Peace Corps medics and treated all of the Afghan villages within fifty miles.

5

The next morning, before sunrise, I woke to the sound of heated voices.

"Why can't I come too?" Toshi asked.

"We are going out to secure the village," replied Mahmoud as he prepared his men for a short patrol.

"I came to Afghanistan to fight! I passed your test the other night!"

"You have proven to me that you can be in my camp, but you have not yet proven that you can handle yourself in a gun fight. When the other men see that you are able, you can come with us. A wedding party will be arriving from neighboring Laghman province this afternoon, please help prepare for our guests, Mazar will tell you exactly what is needed."

"I'm not here to slave for you! After all of the equipment I've given you! I want to fight! You're trying to rip me off! I won't have it!"

"You should not be in such a rush," said Mahmoud with the utmost patience, "you do not even know who you are fighting yet, I know you are an honorable man, I am not trying to rip you off. Thank you for all of the equipment. You must stay here, and if you do not want to help with the preparations, that is fine."

Toshi was still red in the face, but he backed off and stood by the burnt out fire.

"I am sorry," he said, "I kind of lost it for a minute. I suppose I am a little stressed from traveling the last few days. Of course I will help."

I had suspected that Toshi was a little high-strung; I knew that Mahmoud was probably right about him being in a rush. As we stood there with the sun peeking over the horizon, a weird cawing bird sound came from behind us. We turned to look, and it was a hen, crowing like a rooster!

"Oh, that is real bad luck—a crowing hen," Mazar said, and he ran up and smashed it flat with a shovel. There was a big smile on his face.

"What's that all about?" I asked.

"Well, I was really just trying to lighten the mood, I did not want Toshi to be upset all day. A crowing hen is bad luck though I am not really superstitious, the others here would have stayed inside all day if they had seen that."

After tea, Mazar, Toshi and I, along with a few of the other men in the village, began setting up for the party.

First we dug four cooking pits and built two outdoor ovens, then we put up a two meter cloth fence around them, to give the women some privacy during the festivities.

"Two sisters, fifteen and seventeen, from Khas Dawlat Shah, are to be married to brothers, twenty-three and twenty-nine, here in Sra Kala," Mazar said as we worked, "the betrothal, or Kwezhndam, was arranged by the four parents. That is how it works in Pashtun Society, the bride and groom are not involved at all. In most cases, they have never met. The father of the grooms struck a deal with the father of the brides over bride-price, or Walwar."

I suppose an arranged marriage might seem a little old-fashioned to some at the end of the twentieth century. But it wasn't that different from my grandfather's story about his first wedding, his parents had arranged that marriage too; he and his bride had never met before either, and she was also about ten years younger than him. His father presented the bride's father with three fine ponies and five rifles as payment.

A few hours later, the wedding party guests started to arrive. The first to ride in, on well-groomed stallions, was a group of more than seventy-five men dressed in white. They all had heavy gray-black beards and wore purple turbans, and all carried ornately jeweled sabers attached to rich leather belts.

Next came five or six mule drawn wagons each filled with a dozen or so shrouded figures, robed head to toe in dark blue velvet. Surrounding the wagons were about a hundred younger men, eighteen to thirty years old, armed with kalakovs.

I thought of an exchange I had with Pik before I left Hong Kong, "Be careful about how you look at Afghan women," he said, "on second thought, it might be a better idea to not look at them at all. The men, especially Pashtun men, are extremely protective of their females."

I rolled my eyes at him.

"Don't give me that, Jack!! I'm just telling you… I know you can take care of yourself, and I know you're not stupid. I just don't want any problems."

He had told me what to expect, and so I knew the shrouded figures were women. The children and the elderly brought up the rear, in wagons pulled by oxen.

"The bridal procession or Janj, friends and relatives of the brides, could be more than three hundred," said Mazar, "and they will camp next to the village for three or four days of celebration."

The shrouded figures went directly into the women's tent.

"Once inside the tent, the women will take off those burkas," he said.

"This time of year when it's cool," I said, "maybe wearing the burka thing isn't so bad, but what about in the summer? I bet those things are hot as hell, it seems pretty oppressive to make them wear those things."

Toshi shot me a warning look. "They are con-forming to Islamic Law," he said quickly, trying to prevent a fight.

Mazar didn't seem offended. "Yes and no, not all Muslims share the same views on gender segregation. The prophet Mohammed, peace be upon him, always preached about the need for a more egalitarian society."

I waited until Mazar got called away to ask Toshi what egalitarian meant.

"Equal rights for men and women."

Mahmoud came back as we were finishing the setup. He had placed sentries at several points around the village, and plotted escape routes into the Wach Bandar Mountains to evade a sudden attack of the Hind gunship, and then he paid his respects to the Chief of Khas Dawlat Shah. Throughout the night, he stayed in contact with his security team over the two-way radios that Toshi had brought.

Since it was so late by the time the guests had finished arriving, the women made a small meal of baked goat and rice. I'd been working all day, and after I finished eating, it was time to go to sleep. I made my way to our quarters.

"Don't worry Jack," Mazar called after me, "the party will begin tomorrow."

When I got to the little house, Toshi was already asleep inside.

6

The celebration picked up the next afternoon. They did a circular dance called a Khattak that looked kind of like the hokey-pokey with swords, accompanied by clapping and chanting, with a heavy rhythmic beat supplied by three drummers sitting in the center of the circle. The dancers were all men; as I looked around, I didn't see any young women, just elderly women and little girls.

By early evening, two of the visiting men came out of the male tent. The taller one carried a large cotton bag, tied at one end; the other led a ferret like critter on a rawhide leash. A circle of the partygoers formed around the men, the two of them squared off with about two meters between them. The big guy un-wrapped the bag and poured out a two meter long, dark brown snake that reared up and spread its neck into a black hood.

"Kala-Nag, Kala-Nag..." the crowd chanted.

"Kala-Nag is the Oxus cobra," Mazar explained.

Once the ferret, I guess it was actually a mongoose, saw the cobra, it directed its full attention to the reptile, and the handler untied its leash—the fight was on. It seemed unfair to me, the little mongoose looked freaked out, probably from all the people around it, cheering and taunting. The cobra, like most other snakes, was deaf to the noise of the crowd and could concentrate better on getting a good bite in.

Toshi stood beside me.

"I've seen a few of these fights before," he said, "in the mountains of Okinawa, and they always end the same."

"Don't tell me!" I said, knowing the winner would be the snake.

Toshi didn't spoil it for me, he just stood with his arms crossed, watching and smiling.

The cobra towered over the little rodent, and swayed back and forth, as if trying to hypnotize it.

The mongoose hugged the ground with his head angled up pointing at the cobra.

I started feeling sorry for the little guy, thinking that I would much rather be mauled by a long skinny rat, than stabbed by two poison filled hypodermic needles.

Just then, the snake hit the mongoose in the chest. The crowd went silent, and the fight stopped.

The cobra just stood there, it seemed to be waiting for the mongoose to curl up and die or something, but he didn't.

Instead, with lightning quickness, the mongoose darted around behind the cobra's hood, and sunk its little teeth into the back of the reptile's head and shook it mercilessly until it went limp.

The crowd went wild, and I couldn't believe my eyes, a cobra bite could kill four men, a cobra envenomates eighty-five percent of the time when it strikes. I guess Toshi could see the look of disbelief on my face.

"The Mongoose has a natural resistance to cobra venom," he said, leaning over to me.

I'm sure he could see my shock.

"What?!" I couldn't believe I'd never heard that before. "That's not fucking fair!" I blurted.

Nobody noticed.

"Normally, at a Pashtun wedding," Mazar was telling me, "the wedding party holds a contest to find the best marksman, but I don't know if our circumstances will allow it today."

"Gunfire may attract attention from the Soviets," Mahmoud said to the chiefs.

Even though he was only a military commander, they took his advice and announced that due to the current situation, "Ya Naksha Wishtal," no target practice.

There were a lot of disappointed men and boys, but I agreed with Mahmoud, gunfire would surely be noticed.

Toshi saved the day by bringing out three long-bows, five short-bows and six quivers of target arrows. Many of the boys and some of the men had never seen a bow and arrow before. Toshi gave them a demonstration. He motioned for one of the boys to put a big red apple in front of the rifle target, which was about fifty meters from where he was standing.

Then with the group of boys gathered around him, and the men hanging back, he took one of the longbows, knocked an arrow and took a wide stance, with the left side of his body facing the target. Slowly, he took a deep breath, turned his head toward the apple, and with the precision of a well practiced routine, raised the bow until the arrow pointed straight-up.

While exhaling, he lowered it bringing the shaft inline with his eyebrow, and at the same time pulled the bowstring, with the first three fingers of his right hand, back past his ear. He held for a moment, at the full draw and then released. The arrow pierced the apple through its center. The circle of boys gave a muffled gasp, and their eyes got big like they'd just witnessed magic. Toshi pulled another arrow from the quiver and did it again, this time splitting the shaft of the first arrow. His second shot even startled some of the men.

After the demonstration, everyone wanted to shoot the bow. With Toshi coaching, and Mazar translating, the boys formed several groups. The boys used the short bows, and the men used the longbows. A water melon sat on top of a two meter high post as a target.

For the first hour of practice, the boys placed their watermelon posts only about three meters away.

"This will get you concentrating on your draw, the most important aspect of archery," said Toshi.

The men of course started right off trying to hit Toshi's fifty meter target. None did.

The boys shared for almost two hours, but then started fighting over the bows. Finally, the men took the bows and the arrows away from them so they could practice that fifty meter shot. Toshi talked them into moving the watermelons closer, to about twenty-five meters away. Still no one hit it.

I suppose it's odd that I'm part Indian and was raised on the Pine Ridge Reservation for my first eleven years by my full-blooded grandfather, but I never picked up a bow until I was twenty.

In Ranger special weapons training, I had a few weeks of occidental archery, and learned how to make a bow and arrows so that I'd be able to hunt for survival. But I never used that skill, and I hadn't tried to shoot a bow and arrow since then.

So just to see if I could still do it, I took a turn with a longbow and set up the twenty-five meter melon target. Instead of Toshi's expert draw technique, I used my thumb and index finger to pinch the tail of the arrow against the string, and I only drew back as far as my cheekbone. I didn't hit the melon, but it was close enough for me.

By early evening, after the women had been

cooking all-day, it was time to eat. They made a dish called Penda, a chicken dish with Pashtun pasta, chopped onions, garlic, tomatoes, and potatoes, covered in a warm yogurt sauce.

"Penda means a lot in Pashto," said Mazar.

It definitely was, I had three big servings, and finished up on dried apricots, almonds and a cup of tea.

7

The third day of the wedding party was the same as the first two, with the men singing and dancing, the women cooking, and the children playing games.

The boys wrestled each other, and played a chase game; holding one foot up behind themselves and hopping around on the other. The girls played indoors.

The party broke up soon after the evening meal. The men retired to their tent, and the women to theirs. The night was cool and clear. For a while, the evening star was right next to a waxing crescent moon.

"That's an omen of good-fortune," said Mazar.

Then some of the most beautiful singing I've ever heard came from one of the houses in the village.

"The songs, called sandaras, are poems retelling

stories of bravery in battle, or offering praise to the two grooms, for some valiant deed they've done. The singers, all female, are from the bride's family."

When the singing ended, the small group of singers was escorted by a few of their male family members back to the door of the women's tent. Three elderly women, carrying what looked like a bucket of tomato sauce, followed them in. They didn't have an escort, and weren't wearing burkas or veils. Mazar must've seen my question coming.

"Usually only women of marrying age, fifteen to forty years, will be escorted or covered in public. Those women," he pointed to the group of elderly women, "will oversee the bridal Mehndi ceremony, which is similar to a bridal shower in the West. They sing traditional songs, dance the Atanrh, and eat sweets and desserts. No men are allowed. One of the elder women will oversee the braiding of the two brides' hair into three or four plaits. The braiding of hair is meant to bring good luck and fertility to the marriage.

The woman doing the braiding is often the mother of three or four male children. The other two women will oversee the application of the henna dye to their hands and feet."

Toshi and I stayed inside for most of the next day. No one asked us to, but we thought they might like some privacy for the wedding ceremony. When the sun first came up, I went out to get a gallon of drinking water and a loaf of bread for our breakfast. After that we played cards, and Toshi told me some more of his story.

"I was born in Tokushima, Japan, July 6, 1945, two hundred kilometers southeast of Hiroshima, and I assume you know what happened in Hiroshima on August 6th of the same year."

I nodded, after spending so many hours talking to World War II vets, I knew exactly what happened, America dropped the Atom Bomb on Hiroshima.

"Well, my father was a Major in the Emperor's Army. In the middle of October, 1944 he lost his left leg from the knee down fighting in the Ormoc Valley on Leyte Island in the Philippines.

"Despite his humiliation, he was back in Hiroshima by the first week in November. My mother, who had been notified of his injury, was waiting anxiously for him. Obviously, since I was born nine months later, losing his leg didn't affect his virility too much.

"Once disabled, the army transferred him from his combat role to an administrative position in downtown Hiroshima. During her pregnancy, and after I was born, my mother stayed with her parents in Ikumi Beach, Tokushima, and my father commuted back and forth. He was in Hiroshima on the day of the bombing, and somehow miraculously survived inside a collapsed building.

"When she saw the mushroom, my mother left me with my grandparents, and rushed to search for him. She dug through the rubble for three days before finding him."

By the time he talked himself out, and I beat him at every card game I knew, it was late afternoon. I poked my head out to see what was what, and the whole village, including the guests, was gathered around the tables for the evening meal. The food smelled good and I started thinking about eating too. Just as I sat down to whip Toshi at another game of gin rummy, in came Mazar leading the grooms, who carried two heaping plates of chow.

"It's called Sray Karhay Charga, it is baked chicken with lemon juice masala and a yogurt sauce," he said.

The two didn't speak any English, so Mazar translated our thanks and best wishes. He hung back a minute when they left.

"Don't worry," he said, "the women made it. It's another tradition for the bridegrooms to serve the Wedding Feast."

8

The wedding celebration came to a close and the guests were slowly getting ready to head back. Mahmoud was waiting to speak with one of the other mujahideen group leaders from Laghman province, when he came to me.

"Mazar wants to go back to Peshawar," he said, "but I can't leave yet. Jafir will drive, will you and Toshi accompany them?"

"Sure we will," I said.

I didn't ask Toshi first, but remembered a few days earlier, when he was raring to fight. I told him, and he ran back to our house at top speed, disappearing inside. He returned a minute later with his assault rifle and a satchel full of 35-round magazines, and jumped in the back of the truck. I had my 870 and a .45, and rode up front with Mazar and Jafir.

"How come you're going to Peshawar," I asked

Mazar a few minutes out of Sra Kala.

"I live there, with my Mother, and take classes at Islamia College. I have a test tomorrow," he replied.

"Oh. How old are you?"

"I will be nineteen years old on my next birthday. Why do you ask?"

"I just thought the way Mahmoud treats you with so much respect you had to be older."

His full beard threw me off too.

He smiled, and so did Jafir.

"Mahmoud is my father."

"Then, your mother and Mahmoud are divorced? Or were they married?"

"No, I mean yes, they're married. Divorce is almost unheard of in Afghanistan. My mother is the administrator for the Afghan Orphanage and Refugee Center in Peshawar. The Soviet war has driven many out of Afghanistan and it has also made many orphans.

"Before the invasion, my mother, father, and I lived in Kabul, I was born there.

"For many years, father worked as a carpenter and then he got the opportunity to go to the University of Kabul to study veterinary medicine. There he met my mother, who had just started a doctoral program in education.

"They say that opposites attract, well my father is Sunni, like most Pashtun, and my mother is Ishmael Shia, and after mother graduated with her doctorate, they were married, and soon after,

I was born. The next year, the Kabul Zoo opened and father graduated with his degree. He got a job with the zoo as an animal trainer to care for the cats. They had a few tigers from Thailand, a few indigenous snow leopards, and a big African lion named Marjan. When I was small, Marjan was my favorite animal there."

It was dark now, and like I said, the headlights were blacked-out; I'm not sure how Jafir could see.

"My grandfather, Mahmoud's father, was Sra Kala's chieftain, he was killed in a Soviet rocket attack. I never met him, but once Mahmoud learned of his death, he left Kabul and came here to help the people of Sra Kala in any way he could.

"Once here, he saw that they needed security, so he became a mujahideen group leader. A short time later, my mother and I moved to Pakistan, so I could finish secondary school, and so she could run the A.O.R.C."

We were about halfway up the Towr Kham road, when a pair of headlights came racing up in the rearview mirror, and then another pair came out from behind the rocks on our left. Two pickup trucks boxed us in and they hollered something through a bullhorn that I didn't understand.

"Sounds like Russians speaking Pashto," said Mazar.

Jafir nodded.

"They're ordering us out of the truck."

"It's your call Jafir," I said while cycling the action on my 1911.

He hollered something to them and put his hands out the window to show he was unarmed.

I set the pistol in my lap, and put my hands up too.

Glancing in the rearview, I saw Toshi crouching down in the bed, and was sure they couldn't see him.

Two of the mujahideen impostors jumped out of the back of the truck behind us with their guns drawn.

All of a sudden, a blinding flash of light and a thick cloud of smoke erupted from the truck-bed. Toshi had thrown a metsubishi–a ninja smoke bomb, and began shooting at them with well aimed bursts.

Jafir jumped out of the truck, and pulled an RPG from behind the seat. He fired, reloaded and fired again at the truck on our left. It immediately burst into flames.

Toshi kept up with the Galil until the truck behind us was quiet too. They had managed to get a few shots off, but no one was hit; I didn't fire a shot.

Jafir took a quick look inside what was left of the trucks to make sure their occupants were all dead; he took my shotgun. Moments later it went off, and he came back with a Tokerov, 2 AK-74s,* and an RPG-7 with 3 rockets.

"I think there were four men in each truck, they were Russians," he said and held up a few pieces of blackened Soviet uniform insignia.

We continued to Peshawar, dropped Mazar off and headed back. Toshi rode up front, sitting between me and Jafir.

"I will certainly tell Mahmoud that you have proven yourself in a gunfight," said Jafir.

"Yeah Toshi, you saved our asses!" I added.

He didn't respond.

"Do Soviets pose as mujahideen a lot? Why didn't they just start shooting?" I asked.

We both looked over at Jafir.

"It is not unheard of," he said, "sometimes they do it to cause a fight between groups, and sometimes to capture Afghans for information."

When we arrived back in Sra Kala, it was late, but Jafir went to wake Mahmoud who later came to our house.

"Thank you Toshi for saving my son's life," said Mahmoud, "after sundown tomorrow, we will begin to move to an ambush point along the road between Jalalabad and Kabul, forty kilometers northwest of here, there we will wait for a Soviet convoy, please join us."

Toshi didn't say anything, but gave a slight bow. Mahmoud turned to me.

"It seems we had a spy among the wedding guests. The Soviets have been alerted to your presence. Jafir has told me about the attack, if not for Toshi, they would certainly have killed Jafir and Mazar, and taken you into custody. Capturing an American soldier would be a great propaganda victory for them."

I nodded.

When everyone cleared out to let us get some sleep, Toshi went on and on about how he would never take a gun into combat again.

* *The Soviet weapons designer Antonin Kalashnikov developed the AK-47 assault rifle in 1947; in 1974 he developed a second assault rifle dubbed the AK-74.*

9

Mahmoud, Toshi and the group of mujahideen left the next evening.

"We will be back in two weeks," said Mahmoud.

After the wedding, the villagers were used to seeing me around, and most were very friendly, some spoke English–others I just waved to or smiled at. Mahmoud taught me a few words of Pashto before leaving.

I went to see the boy in the hospital tent.

"Zmarak num Jack day, ze malgary yam," I said, assuring him I was a friend.

The doctor was trying to get him out of bed to exercise, so I took him hiking with me, and we climbed a small hill together. The view from the top was incredible; looking to the north, the snow-covered Hindu Kush Mountains seemed to take up the whole sky. After about fifteen or twenty

minutes of daydreaming about them, I gave Zmarak a piggyback ride back to the village.

Back in Sra Kala, I was surprised to see that
Mahmoud and the others were back. I thought
maybe something had gone wrong.

"Even though we missed the convoy, the mission wasn't a complete waste of time," said Jafir,
"Toshi engaged five Soviets by himself."

Toshi had already gone back to our house, so I
asked Jafir to tell me the story.

"It was a cold and windy morning," he began, "we
were perched on the edge of a one hundred meter
cliff about two hundred fifty meters from the road.
A lone KAMaz was pulled off the road right in
front of us."

He paused and looked at me, I had brushed
up on Soviet military vehicles before I left Hong
Kong, so I knew that the Ural-4320 KAMaz truck
was similar to the U.S. Army's M-35 deuce and a
half truck. When he saw that I understood what
he was talking about he continued.

"It was parked on the side of the road, with its
passenger side facing us. Mahmoud studied it with
binoculars, 'Tayr hawa ne leri,' he said. Then he
turned to Toshi and repeated 'the tire is flat.'

"There were three soldiers in the cab, and two
others in the back. Toshi told Mahmoud he'd take
the five alone. Mahmoud agreed, and he was off.

Instead of taking the path down the backside

of the cliff, Toshi climbed down a tree growing next to the cliff-face, and sprinted toward a rock formation that lay approximately twenty-five meters from the truck. Mahmoud motioned for Khaleed and Hiam to follow him.

"I watched him run, with two swords strapped on his back and his bow and a bundle of arrows slung over his shoulder. He is very fast," he smiled, "he reached the rocks before Khaleed and Hiam were even half way there.

"Turning my binoculars to the KAMaz, I saw the two soldiers come out of the back. Both had kalakovs slung over their shoulders, and were carrying the repair tools, vehicle lift and tire wrench. The other three stayed in the cab, but rolled down the passenger window to give instructions or something…I couldn't hear. The two returned to begin working on the right rear wheel.

"Finally Hiam and Khaleed caught up, they ducked down next to Toshi. He was down on one knee and had the bow drawn back, pointing at one of the soldiers.

Just then Mahmoud made a startled sound, and I looked up to see a huge plume of black smoke rising in the distance–maybe thirty-five kilometers away, directly over the road. Then a low rumble echoed off the cliff we were on. The column that we missed was getting hit after all.

"I looked back to Toshi, and he had lowered the bow. The Soviets had abandoned their flat-tire, and moved to the front of the truck, perhaps to see what was happening. The other three soldiers from the cab joined them.

Then the sound of a helicopter approaching from behind got my attention, I looked up in time to see a Hind flying in the direction of the smoke. It was too high, and going too fast to see us.

"Toshi used the diversion to run up behind the truck, and climbed up on its canopy. And when the Soviets turned back, he laid flat so they wouldn't see him. The same three soldiers climbed back in the cab while the two designated tire changers leaned their rifles against the truck, and again took up the tools.

"The two were bent over, each working a tire wrench. Toshi stood up, stepped closer to the edge of the roof, drew both swords and turned around.

Facing away from us with a sword in each hand, he jumped down between them, cutting off both their heads as he landed.

Before the bodies slumped to the ground, he slipped the sword in his right hand over his shoulder into a scabbard, and rolled under the truck.

"The wrenches hitting the ground alerted the others who then exited the truck: two from the passenger side, and the driver from his.

"The two had pistols on their belts, but didn't draw them. I'm sure they saw their headless comrades lying in front of them, maybe they were too shocked to react, I don't know.

"As they neared the bodies, Toshi rolled out from under the truck behind them, and with both hands plunged his sword into the closest man's lower back.

"The sword went through him and came out his stomach. He let out a yelp, and turned around so fast it pulled the sword out of Toshi's hands.

"Toshi quickly drew the sword on his back straight up, stepped forward and brought the blade down on the impaled Soviet's collarbone and slashed downward to where the tip of the other sword protruded.

"The mortally wounded soldier just stood there for a moment, looking down, and then he fell over.

"The next soldier in line drew his pistol. With his left hand, Toshi reached down to his beltline and took, what through the binoculars looked like a long carpenter's nail, and threw it underhand from the hip.

"The soldier grabbed his throat with his left hand, and the pistol in his other hand went off. The shot missed, and Toshi moved in closer and swiped his sword across the man's stomach. His guts fell out. He was dead before he hit the ground.

"Then the driver ran around the end of the truck with a kalakov pointed at Toshi's head, but before he could fire, Toshi went low and kicked the man's legs out from under him.

"He fell over backwards, shooting into the sky, and Toshi stabbed him through the chest before he landed.

"When the fighting was finished, Khaleed and Hiam, went over to admire Toshi's handiwork and to loot the truck, but it was empty so they took the weapons the soldiers had on them."

It sounded pretty impressive. Later, I went back to our quarters to get Toshi's side of the story, but when I got there he was doing some kind of meditation with candles and incense burning, so I didn't bother him.

10

Sitting in the Lotus position, amidst the haze of the burning makko, sandalwood incense powder, Toshi rubbed the dzuko, scented ointment used for spiritual purification, into his palms and remembered the day's events. His father's words echoed in his head.

"Killing with a firearm is cowardly, killing with a sword is honorable."

The time he spent learning the sword came back to him; it was his seventeenth birthday, he and his father stood in the center of the small bamboo forest that his father had been cultivating since Toshi was five.

Both were wearing black umanori hakama, the traditional divided dress-like trousers, with a gray linen montsuki, long-sleeved robe-shirt, tucked in.

They wore white split-toe tabi socks under the leather thonged, rubber-soled, flip-flop like zori. His father, Hitoshi, wore only one, on his right foot; the wooden prosthetic leg he wore on the left, was hidden by the hakama. But his father walked on the prosthesis without limping, and never showed any outward sign of the handicap. His fortitude awed Toshi, and inspired him to excel at every task his father put before him.

"Today you will begin your journey toward manhood, you must no longer play with the kendo sword of your childhood," his father said. "This," he motioned to his right, "is a Katana that has been in the Ushido family for eight generations. Today, it is yours."

Beside them, on the folding table his father had brought into the bamboo garden, lay two Japanese swords. Toshi recognized one of them as his father's brown leather handled military sword—the Katana given to officers in the Emperor's Army during World War II; the other was an old katana wrapped in a purple sash.

The older man took his sword from the table, and slid the end of its scabbard with the blade upside down through his top belt, on his left side.

"You must learn iaido, the drawing and resheathing of the sword."

He gave an embu, demonstration of the basic standing form, and a slight bow to his son. Then Hitoshi quickly moved his left hand to grip the saya, or scabbard, just below the guard where the blade enters it, and with an expressionless face and blank eyes staring straight ahead, he moved his right hand across his body to the hilt, to draw the sword.

Still holding the saya firmly with his left hand, he continued to extend his right arm until the blade was free. Then moving his left hand to join the right, he took a double handed grip on the sword's handle and sliced the air with a short chop, "shwittt." He ended in a defensive stance with the blade's edge down, and point forward.

He held the pose for a few seconds, and then moved his left hand back to raise the scabbard up, while his right arm extended the sword vertically, point-up, flipping the blade over and then bringing it across his body, once again, to rest the spine of the blade right underneath the guard, on the mouth of the scabbard's opening.

Then, pulling the blade's entire length, hilt to point, along the opening of the scabbard–as if cleaning it off, he inserted the point into it, and pushed the sword in up to its hilt. He let both arms fall to his sides, and gave Toshi another slight bow.

"Practice this iaido for a while...but remember, do not touch the blade with your fingers... and never use the sword to cut objects with, as you would a knife, a sword is sacred."

Some time has passed. Toshi and his father are in the bamboo garden again. Both are dressed the same as before, and both are wearing katanas on their left sides.

"Show me the iaido that you have been practicing."

Toshi stepped through the eishin ryu that his father had demonstrated for him on his birthday; his performance was an almost perfect balance of grace and precision. Toshi didn't see it, but Hitoshi was very impressed.

Then, the older man produced a blindfold.

"You must be able to do the iaido without sight."

Hesitantly, Toshi took the blindfold, and fixed it over his eyes; he bowed slightly, and attempted the routine blindly.

This time his loss of vision handicapped him severely; he fumbled both the draw of the blade, and the resheathing. He knew he had not done well, and hung his head in shame.

"Don't worry Toshi," his father said, "iaido takes many years to master. You are doing quite well. You should keep practicing with the blindfold, but you are ready to progress to the most important level of swordsmanship.

"It is called battojutsu: sometimes iaido and battojutsu are used interchangeably, but as the former focuses on the drawing and resheathing of the sword, the later focuses on cutting. How the blade cuts depends on several factors; of course we are assuming that the blade is live–very sharp…but the other factors include the angle of the blade, and the direction and speed of the force behind it.

"This is called toyama ryu, it is a 'cut on the

draw' style that was taught primarily to Army Officers during the war."

Stepping away from his son, Hitoshi centered himself a few feet in front of three bamboo stalks, each a few feet away from the next. He gave the traditional bow, and began.

Except for turning the sword in its case, edge-down, the toyama ryu didn't look much different from the eishin ryu iaido, until the sword was free of its saya.

Then instead of remaining stationary, Hitoshi lunged towards the trees; at the same time extending his sword arm forward, cleanly cutting through the bamboo stalk on the far right. Then tracing the number eight in the air, he reversed the blade making an upward slice through the middle tree.

He continued fluidly with a one-handed downward slice that toppled the third tree, bringing the sword back down to his side, where he again slid the blade from hilt to tip across the mouth of the saya, and finally resheathed it. Ever mindful of etiquette, Hitoshi then gave Toshi another slight bow.

"Iaido treats drawing the sword, and engaging an enemy as two separate functions, battojutsu combines them into one."

Again, some time has passed, three years. Now Toshi is twenty years old. In the middle of the bamboo garden, is a small circle of twelve trees. Hitoshi planted them fifteen years ago, for just this moment.

The diameter of the circle is two meters. At the very center of the bamboo ring, Toshi is sitting in deep meditation.

"When you are focused," his father had told him thirty minutes earlier, "begin."

Toshi opened his eyes, and launched himself up into the Horse defensive position.

Both hands went for the sword, his left hand below the hilt to grip the saya, raising and pivoting the handle forward to meet his right hand. He pulled the sword from its scabbard and extended his arm directly in front of him so the blade was only inches from the first tree.

He moved continuously, leaning forward and slashing downward, severing the bamboo stalk effortlessly.

Turning to the right, with an upward slash, he severed that stalk too. Moving around the circle, in a clockwise direction, he alternated between the downward and upward slashes until he reached the sixth tree—at the six o'clock position.

Then reversing directions, spun back to sever the trees at twelve o'clock and eleven o'clock. He paused momentarily, until the trees had fallen, and then continued with the same alternating upward slash, downward slash to cut the four remaining trees.

As the trees fell, he resheathed his sword, and gave a slight bow to his father.

Back in the present, he looked at his sword, still the same one he was given more than twenty years ago.

His mother had been very upset about Hitoshi giving it to him, but he didn't know why. He overheard a fierce argument between his mother and his father, something about the sword's history that his mother was worried about.

It was the only argument he ever heard his parents have, but Hitoshi dismissed it as superstition, and gave him the sword anyway. He never told Toshi the story of the blade, but left him to find out about it on his own.

The sword maker's signature had been ground-off long ago, making it very difficult to find out anything about it. And Toshi soon forgot about it for a time, going about his training.

Not until after his mother's death, and his own subsequent withdrawal from the Martial Arts, did he find out the sword's history, or its possible history.

At the University in Tokyo, Toshi went to the library and compared a photograph of his family's sword to the photograph of one in the Tokyo antiquities museum. The museum's sword had been made by the legendary fourteenth century swordsmith, Muramasa Senzo, the swords were identical.

In his time, Muramasa was thought to be an alchemist witch, or a metallurgical wizard, and his blades were said to be possessed by a bloodthirsty demon that often drove their owners to fight, and sometimes even cut themselves just to draw blood.

Forged of such high-quality steel, Muramasa blades were said to inspire great fear in the hearts of the Tokugawa shogunate; for this reason, the clan sought to destroy as many of the demon swords as they could. To guard against this destruction, the owners of Muramasa swords often scratched off the smith's signature.

At the time, Toshi didn't think much about the revelation; it seemed too wild and superstitious. But now he wondered…

11

It was late November and getting cold, but the ground wasn't frozen yet.

"It is time to plant the poppies," said Mahmoud.

It seemed like a strange time of year to be planting seeds.

"The poppies will grow well in the cold, dry, winter air," he assured me.

There were farmers to do the planting, but Mahmoud wanted me to become familiar with the crop fields and such. When harvest time arrived, I would pull a round-the-clock guard detail for the plants to protect them from being stolen by rival mujahideen groups.

Toshi, Mahmoud, Khaleed, Jafir, Mazar, and I left early one morning, taking one of 4x4s.

"None of the farmers speak English so Mazar will translate for you, he is also good with numbers and will give you an estimate of the expected opium yield," said Mahmoud.

The fields were not far from the village. Mahmoud dropped Mazar, Toshi and me off in front of a small house that a family of farmers lived in.

"We are going to meet with a man who lives over the next hill, be back in a few hours," he said.

The grow fields were cut into the side of a low mountain, the high side being to the north.

"The naturally sloping mountain provides adequate drainage for the crop. The quickest way to damage the poppies is to let them sit in water," said Mazar.

A wagon load of people met us there, and they went right to work. First they cleaned up the field by clearing weeds and straightening out the aisles. Then working in three husband and wife teams, the man pushed the plow, and the woman guided it while using a long thin stick to poke small holes in the soil every half meter for the seeds.

Mazar talked with them while taking notes.

"Here there are ten, ten acre fields set aside for the poppies," he said.

Mahmoud came back with the others in the afternoon, and frowned when he saw me trying to help.

"This is their job, and they have their way of doing it, so let them. Concentrate on how you will guard the poppies. When harvest nears, Jafir and Khaleed will assist you."

"I've already determined the setup," I said, "we

put two dushkas on the south facing side of the mountain, at the east and west ends, watching for a ground attack, and I'll be on the hill to the south, also with a belt-gun and an RPG..."

"If rival mujahideen groups attempt to steal the crops," interrupted Mahmoud, "we will fight back, but if Soviets come for the poppies, we cannot fight back. I am sorry, but I will not risk Sra Kala. We cannot leave any artillery pieces, not even small-arms, out in the fields. I do not want to attract Soviet attention."

I didn't argue with him because I knew that Mahmoud would not be argued with, and I also remembered in Vietnam, how the U.S. Army dealt with civilian farmers suspected of aiding the VC. He was right.

As evening approached, Mahmoud and the others left again.

"We are going back to Sra Kala, we will come back in a few hours, they will be finished and we will take Mazar back to Peshawar. Wait here, eat something."

Toshi and I built a fire and stoked it with two or three good-sized log stumps. One of the farmers, an elderly woman named Malala, prepared a meal of chicken and beets.

Earlier in the day, one of the Afghan farmers had given me a small pipe and a little chunk of opium. It was dark brown and sticky, looked like tar-hash.

It had been a few months since I'd gotten high

on the beach in Hong Kong, and I was more than ready. I offered some to Toshi, and he reluctantly took it. He took a giant hit and coughed most of it back out.

It occurred to me, that he had never gotten high before. "Whoa," I said chuckling, " take it easy there shooter."

"I smoked too much!" he blurted, launching up to his feet and looking at me through tear-filled eyes, his face full of panic.

"No, sit down. Calm down man, it's all right."

I smoked the rest of it myself, got pretty baked; my thoughts wandered, and my childhood came back to me.

When I was a kid on the Res, my grandfather had a half-acre plot he grew green beans, carrots, and sweet potatoes on. We usually had good suppers, and enough extra to share with the neighbors too. We had a Billy goat, a bull, two cows, and a few chickens.

I got too comfortable and drifted off.

The sun had vanished and the fire had burned down to embers when Mazar woke me.

"They are finished, here are some figures: there are approximately one hundred acres here," he said, "they planted just over half a kilo of poppy seeds per acre, and expect eighteen plants per square meter, there are a little more than four thousand square meters per acre. Yield should be nine kilos of opium per acre, nine hundred kilos in total which will produce ninety kilos of heroin.

"This crop will be ready to harvest by the middle of March or early April. For the first two and a half months, the plants must be well tended to avoid damage from overwatering or freezing, as well as insect and fungal attack. Of course, grazing animals must be kept away from here. When the plants are one meter tall, they won't require as much attention."

Later that night, the six of us drove back to Peshawar to drop off Mazar, we spent the night at the home of some friends of Mahmoud's.

The next morning, at about seven-thirty, Toshi and I went looking for breakfast, and then spent the rest of the day wandering around the congested Storyteller's Bazaar, being assaulted by the pungent odors, and eating goat kebabs. Mahmoud and the others went to the mosque to meet with a few other mujahideen group leaders and tribal chieftains.

As evening approached, Jafir and Khaleed found us in the Dean's Restaurant drinking tea. They introduced us to a Pakistani named Hassam who was joining Mahmoud's group.

"Mahmoud says we will stay in Peshawar for another night, at the home of Khaleed's uncle, and return to Sra Kala before sunrise," said Jafir. "Mahmoud is still at the mosque, but will join us shortly."

That night we met Khaleed's uncle, Ahmet, at his house. He had been a blacksmith before the war, but now earned his living making and repairing weapons for the mujahideen. He had a large family, two wives, three sons, and two daughters and was a very devout Muslim. He strictly kept to the custom of abstaining from alcohol, wine, and every other intoxicant, and prayed toward Mecca six times a day.

Even though he talked about his wives and daughters as any proud husband and father would, I only saw one of his wives when she served us a small meal of boiled chicken and rice, she was covered head to toe in a burka.

After supper, I picked a spot on the floor, in the far corner of the room, and curled up with a blanket. The others stayed up talking in a language I didn't understand.

12

We left Peshawar the next morning before sunrise. I drove, with Toshi next to me and Mahmoud by the window. The others were in the back of the pickup.

Fifteen kilometers out of the city we started climbing the Jamrud-Kyhber Road.

The sky in front of us still had that early dawn look to it, but behind us, it was pinkish. I must've been half asleep, because the next thing I knew we had already crossed the Pakistan-Afghanistan border pass and were on the Afghan side. As we passed the Towr Kham turnoff, the sun started peeking over the mountains behind us.

"You must stop, it is time for the Salaat," said Mahmoud.

"But I'm a Catholic, and I think Toshi is Buddhist," I said jokingly.

"Well, no one is perfect," he replied, smiling,

"pull over here."

The four left the truck with their prayer rugs, crossed the unpaved road, unrolled them on the ground, and facing west-southwest, away from the sun, knelt on both knees. With their arms spread out in front of them, palms down, the men pressed their foreheads to the rugs, holding their heads to the ground for a few seconds, then sat up all as one, and repeated the bow. The window was rolled down a slit, and I could hear them begin to chant something.

"They're speaking Arabic," said Toshi.

It had to be cold, I could see their breath. Then, feeling like maybe I was invading their privacy, I looked the other way.

Suddenly, I heard something in the distance. From his reaction, I think Toshi must've heard it too, the far-off droning of a big helicopter. I couldn't see it, but the sound was getting louder. I was sure the others could hear it now.

I jumped up onto the hood of the truck to check out the sky with the binoculars and saw it as a point, north of us, flying west-southwest across the wide open plain.

The chopper was still about eighteen kilometers away, and I didn't think its crew could see us yet. But I knew it had to be an Mi-24 Hind…with a few 12.7 mm machine guns, almost two-hundred 57 mm unguided rockets, and four or five two hundred fifty kilogram napalm bombs.

Please don't see us…

Just then, it turned south and flew directly towards us.

Shit!

I turned to look at Mahmoud and the others, but they were still praying.

I jumped down from the hood, and hopped into the truck. Luckily, the engine sprang to life right away.

The Hind was closing in, but they still didn't move from their prayers.

"We have to get them, now!" Toshi yelled when the chopper was less than ten kilometers away,

I definitely agreed, but had been told never to interrupt the Salaat.

Thankfully, they finished. Mahmoud and the others got up, casually rolled up their prayer rugs and threw them in the back of the truck. He motioned for the binoculars, and studied the approaching helicopter.

"I am driving," he said, handing them back to me.

I scooted over next to Toshi, Mahmoud climbed in, and the other three jumped in back. Khaleed and Jafir stood up behind the cab and began to buckle themselves in.

"Knock when you are ready," Mahmoud said through the cab window.

They had two RPG-7s with three rocket grenades each. Mahmoud took off toward the helicopter. Toshi and I were concerned, but we stayed quiet. The speedometer read ninety kilometers per hour.

"Approximately how far away do you think they are? And how fast do you think they are going?" he asked.

In the rearview mirror I could see that Jafir and Khaleed were both facing forward, pointing the RPGs.

"Four kilometers, two hundred kilometers per hour, give or take," I said, trying to keep the fear out of my voice.

He floored it, and the truck quickly sped up to one hundred twenty kilometers per hour.

"There are no bases in the northeast. The rocket pods are almost empty and there is only one bomb left. They must be coming back from an early morning attack, probably on the way back to Jalalabad Airbase," said Mahmoud peering straight ahead.

The Hind began firing its remaining S5 Rockets at us. Without slowing down at all, Mahmoud pulled a huge Zigzag pattern; cutting a hard right, until it fired again, and then cutting a hard left. He repeated that maneuver several times, and incredibly we skirted all fifteen of the rockets.

With the looming gunship less then a thousand meters away, Mahmoud punched it again. Even though the ground was flat, the truck was shaking badly.

"We call this helicopter, the devil's chariot," Mahmoud voice rose over the noise of the engine, "RPGs are next to useless against its armor, but the tail rotor assembly is its Achilles Heel. It has fired all of its rockets, and now the only thing to worry about is that bomb. This pilot must be a rookie though, he should already have dropped it."

Not a minute later the pilot dropped the napalm bomb. The Hind was maybe three hundred meters off the ground. I flashed on the time when I was bombed with the marijuana bales in the South China Sea.

I could just make out the pilot's face when Khaleed and Jafir knocked on the roof of the cab, and Mahmoud slammed on the brakes. I braced my arms against the dash, and watched out the top of the windshield as the napalm and the Hind kept going. He'd been planning this all along.

"Pft-pft," sounded the RPGs as they were launched.

Hassam was ready with the reloads, and Khaleed and Jafir fired again.

The first two mini-warheads destroyed the tail-rotor sending the bird into a horizontal spin; the second two severed the tail from the fuselage, and the flying tank fell from the sky.

Mahmoud drove over to where the pieces landed, and Hassam leapt out of the back of the 4x4 screaming wildly.

"Allahu Akbar! Allahu Akbar! Allahu Akbar!"

I think they would've taken the pilot and gunner captive, but they didn't survive the fall. The Hind didn't explode, but it landed pretty hard.

13

It was a few weeks into December, and cold, real cold. Toshi and the mujahideen were gone from Sra Kala–I'm not sure where they were.

It hadn't snowed until the end of November, and I thought about growing up in the Black Hills with grandfather.

"If it snows before the end of October," he used to say, "there will be a lot of snow that winter, but if not it will be a mild winter."

I guess his prediction applied only to South Dakota because it was snowing two or three times a week now, and colder than I'd seen in a long time. I worried that the poppies would get too cold.

"Now that they have had a few weeks to get their roots down, they will be fine, the snow will insulate them from the freezing wind," said one of the English-speaking villagers.

Most days, if it wasn't snowing, I hiked into the

Wach Bandar Mountains in the afternoons; Wach Bandar Ghar was the tallest of the group.

I think it was about the same size as Harney Peak, around three thousand meters. On top I found a good spot to watch the sunset; it was spectacular, the orange red globe shining its fading light over the snow-covered plains.

I didn't want to get stuck in the mountains after dark, so I never watched the ball go all the way down, but started walking back to the village about ten minutes into it.

I took Zmarak with me a few times. The doctors said his wounds were healing very well; he didn't wear a bandage on his face anymore, and the stump where his hand used to be wasn't leaking as much.

He didn't speak English, and I only knew a few words of Pashto, but he was good company.

One afternoon as we were heading out of Sra Kala, I noticed a horse sleigh sitting in back of the blacksmith's shop. It was full of snow, and obviously hadn't been moved in quite some time.

The skids were removed, and left leaning against the side of the chassis. They were almost three meters long and a meter wide. I borrowed one, along with a set of leather reins that were lying on top of the bench seat.

I'm sure he wondered why I would carry it up the mountain, but at the top, I lashed the skid to my feet, and surfed down.

I could hear him laughing and hollering behind me, as I rode the stationary wave, the cold wind in my face. I thought about all the winter days I skipped school to go skiing or snow surfing; it sure seemed like a long time ago.

When I got to the bottom, I took the skid off and walked back up the mountain. He ran over to me with his arms outstretched, all grins and teeth, jabbering something. I reattached the board, lifted him up on my shoulders, and got ready to ride down the long gentle slope again, he was hooting in my ear the whole time.

By the end of January, Jafir came back to Sra Kala. He said the others were fine, but he had taken some shrapnel in his left leg when a Soviet grenade detonated too close to him.

Mahmoud ordered him back to Sra Kala, he and Khaleed drove one of Toshi's pickups.

After they'd told me what they'd been doing for the last few weeks, they began talking about how they had come to fighting with the Mahmoud.

They also told me a little about Kabul, with its many Soviet military buildings and high-security Officer Housing Compounds, and they said that there were a few mountains surrounding it, and a river that ran through the city.

Both made it clear that they were ready to get back to fighting.

So I mentioned that they should stakeout one of the buildings, and snipe one or more of the high ranking officers going in or coming out. They acted like they'd never heard of such a thing, I wasn't sure if they thought the act of using a sniper was a cowardly way of fighting, or if they just never thought of it before.

I told them about some of the sniping I had done in Vietnam, and they seemed somewhat interested, especially when I told them that by taking out one Soviet General, or some other 'high-value target,' they could score a huge victory for the mujahideen.

They liked that, and pretty soon we were talking about going to Kabul.

I asked if they had some kind of target or hunting rifle, but the only rifles they had were kalakovs. I was sure that Abdullah, in Dara Adam Khel, could make me a Remington model 700 or a Winchester model 70 in a hurry, but we wanted to get going now, before Mahmoud came back from Jalalabad.

Then I remembered the story of Carlos Hathcock, the Marine sniper in Vietnam, and his legendary 2,000 meter shot. He used a Browning M2 .50 cal machine gun fitted with a scope. I thought we could try a similar setup with a dushka 12.7 mm belt-gun. We waited for nightfall, and made a run to Peshawar to get a scope from a friend of Jafir's.

His name was Hiatt; he was a big, round, gray-haired Pakistani who spoke English with that musical-nasally accent I heard on the train through India. He ran a 'junk store' in the Andarsheher Bazaar, and after Jafir prompted me, I told him that we were looking for a scope that could be calibrated for more than a thousand meters.

"Oh yes," he said, "I have just what you need."

He went in the back for a few minutes, and came back with a brand-new Zeiss 10 x 50 millimeter rifle scope.

"Oh, I almost forgot," I said, "we want to mount it to a dushka."

"Oh?" he looked at me like I was crazy, and then looked at Jafir for confirmation; Jafir nodded.

"Well then," he said, "I have a machine shop in the back," he gestured with his head, "I can make a mount for you, it will only take a few minutes."

"Hold on," I said, "I'll go get the gun from the truck, for measurements."

"No," he said nonchalantly, "I have one in the back, I have a little bit of everything here, I can sell you a gold watch or a color television, a mink coat for your girlfriend or a Soviet flamethrower."

I smiled, and he went to work.

Thirty minutes later, he came back with a makeshift scope-mount. I gave him three hundred dollars for the scope and two hundred dollars for the mount.

On the way back to the truck, we stopped for a goat kabob. I was amazed when no one wanted to go to the mosque before we left.

The next day in Sra Kala, we packed food and fuel for the one hundred forty kilometer drive, and I put the scope on the machine gun. The three of us got a few hours of sleep, and left around three o'clock in the morning.

There was a good paved road to Kabul, but it was the Red Army's main thoroughfare across Afghanistan, so we took an old dirt caravan path that was parallel to it.

"We should sight the scope before we get there." I said after about seventy-five kilometers.

"The sun will be coming up in an hour or so," said Jafir, "we will stop soon for the day," he pointed ahead, "up there is a group of hills where you can configure the scope."

I couldn't see the hills he was talking about.

Khaleed had been so quiet thus far, I'd almost forgotten he was even in the truck.

"I know of a place on the outskirts of Kabul," he said, "where we can find one of your 'high-value targets'."

He said something to Jafir in Pashto, and Jafir nodded.

"The Tadzh-Bek Palace," said Jafir, "it was originally the Afghan Royal Family's residence, and for a short time it was the residence of the Communist President of Afghanistan, Amin. I don't know why, but he was executed by the KGB in 1979, and the palace has been the headquarters for the Soviet 40th Army ever since then. it is fifteen or sixteen kilometers from the center of Kabul, and sits at the top of a terraced hill, surrounded by forested foothills. The security there is very high, but the hills should provide adequate cover for two men on foot."

The two spoke a few words in Pashto, then Jafir said that he would go with me, while Khaleed waited in town with the truck.

"Those hills," again he pointed ahead of us, and this time I could make the hills out, "are almost two thousand meters from here." he said as he braked.

I jumped out of the cab, and quickly spotted three large rocks I could use to prop up the large round oven pans I'd gotten in Peshawar. In only a minute or so, I was back in the truck, and we continued to the daylight resting spot on top of the hill.

Just when Jafir killed the engine, I heard the whump-whumping of two big helicopters. We had some good tree cover over us, but stayed in the truck until they flew over. The two Hinds were flying east-northeast.

I'm sure it was below zero, but they grabbed their prayer rugs and were off, leaving me to build a fire and get some tea going. I wished I had a little whiskey.

After a few cups of hot tea, the cold wasn't so biting. I took the machine gun, still on its tripod, out of the bed and set it down in the little clearing where I'd be shooting from.

There's only one shooting mode on a dushka, full auto, so I slid a few 12.7 bullets out of the non-disintegrating belt, so I could load each shot singly.

Once I'd focused the 10 x 50 scope to my eye, I used a pen-light and a tree to bore sight the scope as best I could. Next, using binoculars, I found the oven pan targets I had set up below the hill, and then switched back to the scope. I pulled back the charge lever, inserted the first round, and trained the crosshairs on the black square of electrical tape I put at its center.

I squeezed the trigger, and quickly switched to the binoculars before the gun bucked.

Though the shot hit the pan it was high in the top left, but with about forty-seven left-clicks on the elevation knob and fifty right-clicks on windage, the next two shots pierced the black square on the oven pan.

There were two more oven pans down there, but the scope was set, and I didn't want to give away our position. So I put the gun away, and went back to sitting by the fire. Jafir and Khaleed were back from their morning prayers, and we started planning.

14

Jafir and Khaleed decided that we shouldn't go into Kabul after all.

"It might be dangerous," said Jafir.

Instead we drove south across the paved road and picked up another caravan path going southwest.

"Some twenty kilometers outside of Kabul there is a mountain," he said, "Barghowlay Ghar, on the far side is a small village called Barg-e Gol. The villagers are only farmers, there is no mujahideen group operating there, so Khaleed will drop you and me at the mountain, and then take the truck there to wait for us."

It was slow going on the back roads; I'd insisted that they put chains on the tires before the end of November, and this was the first time I was with them to see the benefits. Without the chains we would've gotten stuck for sure.

We reached the mountain about an hour before sunrise. With no weapons or evidence that he wasn't by himself, Khaleed dropped us off, and agreed to come back after sunset. He then drove on around the mountain to Barg-e Gol. Jafir and I donned snowshoes and walked northeast.

I slung the counterfeit dushka over my right shoulder and my trusty 870 pump over my left. Jafir carried the folded up tripod in a pack, with two pairs of binoculars, a coil of rope, two rappelling harnesses, and enough dried chicken and water to last a day. He also slung a shorty Kalashnikov AK-74 over his shoulder, the Soviets called it a suki, which is Russian for 'little bitch.'

With about seventeen kilometers to the palace, we quietly pulled a light jog through the snow filled forest.

The only thing that kept my legs from freezing was the blood-pumping cadence we kept. I don't think Jafir was having any problem with the snow, but my feet hadn't been so cold since I was a little kid running around in the Black Hills.

As dusk was breaking, we found a group of boulders I thought would be a good shooter-hide. It was maybe three and a half meters off the ground, so I free climbed it first and sent down the rope to bring up the machine gun, the tripod and the other bag of equipment. After I pulled up the stuff, Jafir climbed up.

"I think it will snow today," Jafir said for the third time since Khaleed dropped us off.

It was getting lighter out, but the sky was still pretty gray.

Studying the compound through the binocs, we were about two kilometers away from a south facing entrance that was enclosed by a three meter wrought-iron, razor-wire topped fence with four meter guard towers at either end, and a ram-proof security gate.

Inside the enclosure, next to the main headquarters building, was a barracks complex and what I thought was probably a mess-hall, an ammunition depot and a fueling station.

Not much was going on in the compound, a few troops with dogs patrolling around the fence line, a janitorial crew shoveling snow off a driveway that looped around from the front of the building. At first glance, it didn't seem like there was very much security; then I took a closer look at the guard towers.

There were two of them on the south-side of the compound, but only one of them was facing us directly. I switched from the binoculars to the Zeiss scope for a closer look.

I saw two soldiers inside the tower looking through binoculars in either direction, doing a slow pan. Though it was overcast, I didn't want to take the chance of giving off a scope-flash, so I quickly covered it.

"When I shoot," I said, "the towers will probably see it, and this group of boulders is going to make judging the range very simple for them. I'm sure the sandbag mounds in front of the towers are barricades for mortars, no doubt they're wired to the towers for range estimates...so when I shoot, we'll only have a few seconds to get out of here before they frag this place."

Jafir closed his eyes and exhaled loudly through his nose. He mumbled something under his breath, followed by, "Insha'Allah."

I could almost hear his thoughts.

I didn't really have a plan, was just waiting for an opportunity.

Suddenly, an alarm-bell started ringing, and around thirty-five soldiers, wearing winter-camo fatigues and carrying Kalashnikovs, came running out of the barracks into snow-covered parade grounds and stood at attention in a muster formation.

They were lined up in three rows, front to back, with their backs toward us. In front of them was a drill sergeant, or CO, barking orders.

I thought if I aimed at the center-back of the middle soldier in the last row, I could hit four of them with one shot. Maybe even get three shots off before the first one gets there, then I'd try for the sentries in those towers; thirteen or fourteen casualties, then we'd have to get going.

I told Jafir what I was thinking, and then I reached for the machine gun's ammunition belt. I'd decided that loading each shot individually would be too slow for what I wanted to do.

Noting that the rate of fire, on a dushka, is

around six hundred rounds per minute, it was obvious that the first few shots would demand a trigger pull of less than a fraction of a second—for the sake of accuracy. I flipped up the lens cover on the scope.

It was bitter-cold, so I knew there was little if any humidity in the air to slow the bullet. And there was no wind to contend with.

It was about two kilometers and uphill maybe twenty-five degrees from the hide to the compound, so I found my target and aimed a little high, putting the center of the crosshairs on the midline of the back of his head, and I started to gently squeeze the trigger.

"Wait!" said Jafir.

And I immediately flipped the cover down, and switched to the binocs in time to see a fuel tanker come around the corner of the headquarters building. I guess they were there to refill the pump in front of the depot.

Then I thought, a few shots into the soldiers at formation, then hit that truck and the towers, thirty-plus casualties easy.

I flipped up the lens-cover again, and got set to start shooting.

"Wait, Zil!" Jafir interrupted again.

This time when I pulled the binocs up, a big black car, with little red hammer-sickle flags on the front corners of the hood, was pulling around the corner; it stopped underneath a canopy at the building's rear entrance.

Then the janitorial crew rolled a carpet out over the icy walkway, from the doorway to the passenger door of the limousine.

"Wow, talk about good fortune," I said, "maybe we're going to get some high-value targets after all."

Jafir didn't say anything, but kept looking through his binoculars.

Two uniformed men came to the doorway, one tall and thin, the other short and stocky, both wore black uniforms with visored caps. Short and Stocky's chest was covered with medals, and colorful ribbons, while Tall and Thin didn't have as many medals on his chest.

"A General," said Jafir.

I don't think he could tell for sure at this distance, it was wishful thinking, but I suppose I was thinking the same thing.

Tall and Thin walked towards us across the carpet and opened the limo's rear door. When two more officers got out, and the three of them walked single file back up the carpet towards the General, I reached for the gun and flipped up the lens cap.

Out the side of my mouth, I told Jafir what I was aiming to do, and that he should get ready to run.

With the Last in Line's head in my crosshairs, I squeezed the trigger for that fraction of a second, then turned the gun back to the soldiers in formation and squeezed off another few rounds.

Not stopping there, I put the fuel tanker under the plus sign, and squeezed off a whole second's worth of 12.7 millimeter bullets.

"Four officers down!" said Jafir, with a rush of excitement in his voice.

"And nine soldiers down t—"

A huge explosion cut him off, and the entire compound enclosure was engulfed in thick black smoke. I know it was far away, maybe it was just exhilaration, but for an instant I felt the heat from it.

"You better go now!" I said, "I'm right behind you."

He already had his harness on and forward-rappelled over the edge of the boulder-hide.

I turned back to the scope. I could barely find the tower through all the smoke, and when I finally did the sentries inside were both looking through their binoculars: my way.

I quickly squeezed off the last twenty or thirty rounds of the belt, and heard the "phoomp" that announced an incoming mortar shell. I left the empty-gun, and took a running leap off the three meter high perch.

I landed and rolled on the packed snow just as the top of our nest was obliterated.

"You know they're coming," I shouted, "we'd better beat feet back to Barghowlay Gahr."

Jafir nodded, threw me my snowshoes and 870 pump, and led the way.

Now we were pulling a full-run. I could hear a helicopter coming after us.

Just then the temperature went up slightly, and

it started snowing. At first it was coming down gently, but after ten minutes the wind picked up and it soon became a total whiteout blizzard.

"I don't hear the helicopter anymore," I said.

"No," Jafir replied over the sound of the wind, "they probably could not see, and turned back… we should not stop running though, they might continue the pursuit on foot, or with dogsleds."

Soon the snow was getting deep and really hard to run through. The only thing I could hear was the wind blowing and our footfalls.

"Hold on Jafir," I said, breathing heavy, "I've got to stop for a minute."

I'd lost a snowshoe, and I wanted to take the other one off too.

I dug through my last track and found the one that came off. Then gave them to Jafir, he'd stopped to take his own off and was putting them in the equipment bag he carried on his back.

"We have not eaten anything all day," he said, passing me a few drumsticks and the canteen.

I hadn't realized how hungry I was. I went through those chicken legs in only a second.

"Do not leave any bones," he said, holding out a small brown paper bag.

"I'm sure we've run sixteen kilometers," I said, "that mountain, Barghowlay Gahr, has to be close."

"Yes, we will no doubt be there in less than one hour," he said, "and then we will have another hour before the sun goes down. I think it has almost fin-ished snowing, we should stash our weapons, and continue on to Barg-e Gol to find Khaleed."

By the time we walked in to the village, it had stopped snowing and the sun had just set. It was still twilight and I saw Khaleed sitting, around a fire with a group of farmers. He assured them that Jafir and I were his friends, and that we had no weapons. Jafir showed them that his bag was carrying only an old set of binoculars and a pair of snowshoes, and then he told them they shouldn't worry because we were leaving.

I was so happy to get back in the truck and turn the heater on.

Jafir explained to Khaleed what we'd done, and how we were pursued until the snow fell.

"Now that it has stopped snowing," said Khaleed, "do you not think the Soviets will continue the pursuit? After you have attacked their fortifications? Surely they will not forget that—you should leave those weapons where they are, we will drive south to Khoshi, in Logar province, the Soviets will not look there, it is controlled by the Jamiat e-Islami.

"Once we are there we can take a caravan path back to Sra Kala. It is a slight detour, but will not take that much longer."

While I dozed, Jafir gave Khaleed all the details of our assault. I wasn't completely unconscious, so I could hear him retelling the story; he spoke in English for my benefit. I think Khaleed was impressed.

Though it was dark and I couldn't see much,

Logar was a pretty mountainous region, like most of Afghanistan and Pakistan, and it took almost four hours to get to Khoshi.

We stopped there only long enough for Jafir and Khaleed to say hello to a few friends. They traded us three roasted chickens and a big clay jug of hot tea for our binoculars.

When we got back on the caravan path east, Jafir took over driving for Khaleed, who sat between us and put his head down.

"What is Jamiat e-Islami?" I asked Jafir.

"It is an Islamic religious, political, social organization, it is fairly conservative, somewhat militant." he said.

"I remember Mazar talking about his grandfather being a member of the Jirga," I said, "same thing?"

"Well, a Jirga is a local Pashtun tribal council, Pashtuns are mostly Sunni Muslim. Jamiat, on the other hand, is an international organization started by Persians. Its membership is mostly Shia Muslim. Other than that, I suppose you could say they are similar."

"Didn't Mazar tell me that his mother is Ismaili Shia?"

"Yes," said Jafir, "she is my sister, we are, including Khaleed, Tajiks."

"You are Mazar's uncle? Mahmoud's brother-in-law?"

"Yes," he said.

I figured I would ask about the Tajik thing later.

I already had an idea about the difference between Sunni Muslim and Shia Muslim.

We drove east-northeast the rest of the night, and pulled into Sra Kala as the sun was coming up. Mahmoud wasn't back yet.

15

At the Jalalabad Air Base morgue, Major Ali Hassan Rasullah was examining the remains of five Soviet soldiers that had been recovered from a site not far from the base.

He would report his findings to a Colonel Kringov in Kabul. Though Rasullah wasn't a doctor, but only an Intelligence Officer in the army, he did have some specialized forensics knowledge.

The examining room was not really a morgue at all, but just an un-insulated room in the far corner of the hangar that held the Black Tulips while they were being loaded with their cargo.

Black Tulip is the name given to the Antonov An-12 transport planes by the Red Army soldiers; they carry the bodies of the fallen Soviets home to Russia.

Rasullah was familiar with injuries caused by bladed weapons. And from a cursory examination of the corpses, he concluded that the wounds, a cleanly amputated right arm—the arm itself was found, still gripping a suki, and several severe lacerations and well-placed slashes across the abdomen, and punctures in the upper chest and back, and two decapitations, were made with a blade.

That information, in and of itself, doesn't really mean anything other than exactly what it sounds like: the duhki insurgents are beheading Soviets.

The revelation that Islamic Warriors are chopping the heads off of enemy combatants isn't a new one. But these were not just posthumous battlefield atrocities; the soldiers had no gunshot wounds or evidence of any other battlefield type injuries.

They weren't executions; the bodies were recovered at the same time and location as those that suffered the more common injuries associated with modern warfare, and neither was it the work of simple mountain men insurgents; they were fine, surgical cuts, from a calculated hand.

Such precise cuts could of course have been made with a very sharp knife, he knew, but considering that they were so straight, long and clean, it seemed more likely that it had been a sword.

And the possibility that there could be a trained swordsman, perhaps even a Samurai, fighting in Afghanistan excited him very much.

"The wounds where made with a bladed-weapon, probably a sword." Rasullah said into the telephone receiver.

"A sword?!" Colonel Kringov replied incredulously.

"Yes sir, I am certain of it."

"Certain?! How are you so certain Rasullah?" the colonel implored.

"I have seen these injuries before, sir. At the Mehtar Lam Outpost, I am in charge of intelligence gathering from the captured insurgents. I will not go into it now, but one of my interrogation methods involves the Katana–Japanese Sword."

The line went silent for a moment.

"I've heard of you," Kringov said, "you are the Afghan Executioner?"

Rasullah had heard the nickname before, he did not mind it, he liked its 'ring.'

"I am sir," he replied.

"What do you think should be done about this situation.

"I will deal with this personally," Rasullah said, not wanting to lose the opportunity to face this opponent.

16

It was the end of April, and more than three quarters of the crop was ready to harvest. Mazar had come to translate between me and the farmers. There were plenty of people in Sra Kala, including the farmers and other villagers. But Mahmoud, Toshi, and the others were in western Nangarhar province; they'd been gone for two weeks.

We joined the farmers in the fields the first morning.

"After the full bloom of the flower," Mazar said while holding a poppy that was still attached to its stalk, "its petals begin to fall away. Once all the petals are gone, an egg-yoke shaped sac remains, inside is an off-white sappy goo, this is the opium. Today they will be scoring the pods."

I guess there was a blank look on my face, because Mazar paused and looked at me.

"I will explain. A group of women with thin

bladed knives, will start at the end of the field, and work their way back to its beginning, walking down the rows, to inspect each pod for maturity.

"Mature pods appear slightly swollen and are dark-green in color, they will make a shallow incision down the center of the pod, on both sides, it gets the opium flowing and exposes it to the air so it will thicken. Then tomorrow morning, they will return."

Before the sun came up the next morning, the same group of six women went back into the fields; each carried a filet knife, and a two gallon steel cooking pot. Mazar asked the leader of the group, an old woman named Khatol, if I could watch her for a little while.

Khatol was the woman who did the Mehndi Ceremony at the wedding when Toshi and I first arrived. Mazar said she had been processing opium since her childhood.

We followed her down the last aisle, and she was talking the whole time, but I couldn't understand what she was saying. I guess it was just small talk because Mazar didn't bother translating.

When we came to a scored pod, without damaging or removing the pod from its stalk, she carefully squeezed the opium sap right out of it, kinda squirted out like toothpaste, into her waiting steel pot, and then she moved on to the next one. She said something to Mazar.

"She says, they will continue like this for the rest of the day, and then come back tomorrow morning for a final pass to scrape out any opium that remains."

By late morning, they had finished the initial collection; each woman had filled, emptied, and refilled their steel pots about five times. The first day's collection netted just under four sanitized fifty-five gallon oil drums full of raw opium.

"Khatol says she expects to collect half as much opium tomorrow," said Mazar, "she wants to begin extracting the following day."

There was still a few acres worth to collect, but they'd give it a few days maturing time, and then come back.

We loaded the opium-filled oil drums into a wagon and trucked them into the village where the cooking pits we had dug for the wedding back in November were located.

They covered the bottom of an empty drum with chunks of crushed limestone and heated it until it was approximately the same temperature as a blacksmith's kiln, according to Mazar this made calcium oxide, or quicklime. They then filled the barrel a little more than half-way up with clean water and brought it to a boil, stirring constantly.

I was watching, but Mazar was there to give me a play by play.

"While the mixture is boiling, they will add the opium, and let it continue boiling for an hour, or until the plant matter coagulates, and either sinks to the bottom or is scooped out. Once the barrel is removed from the fire, the solution is covered and left to sit overnight, another empty drum is brought forward, and the process is repeated."

Three days of boiling, stirring, cooling and filtering, stirring some more, adding nushadir salt, a volcanic rock mined near Kabul, and reheating, then re-filtering, rendered about six hundred fifty kilos of pure opium into sixty-five kilos of morphine base.

"The chemists will do the rest," Mazar explained, "since there is really no legitimate use, here in Afghanistan, for the industrial chemical acetic anhydride, it is smuggled from Pakistan. Khatol tells me that three young Pashtun men from the North West Frontier Province will arrive tomorrow morning, they will bring the necessary equipment."

"Do you think we can trust these guys?" I asked.

Mazar looked at me warily.

"I hope so," he said, "the group leader is the son of Sra Kala's chieftain, and I believe the other two are his nephews."

Just Checking.

The three arrived in a pickup truck the next morning before the sun came up. All of their stuff was in the back of the truck: chemicals, plastic tubs, big aluminum pots, giant Bunsen burners with propane tanks, electronic scales, and electric mixers with a gas generator. They spoke English, and said I was welcome to watch them.

"These chemicals put off harsh fumes, it might be uncomfortable if you get too close."

Before starting, they weighed the dried morphine base again, and then weighed out an exact portion of acetic anhydride and mixed it with the base.

Then the morphine went into an aluminum pot full of steaming hot water, and the electric mixers were fired up, mixing it until all of the morphine had dissolved into the water, creating a clear brown solution. They continued mixing it for a few minutes more.

When satisfied with the consistency, the mixer was pulled out and the pot was covered and left to cool for about an hour.

There were about eight batches, a little more than eight kilos per batch, going at the same time. And my eyes were burning pretty good, kind of like the tear gas test from my basic training almost fourteen years ago, but I stuck it out.

"We are almost finished," said the chieftain's son, Hamman, "we will eat lunch now, and return at one-thirty."

The three of them went into the chieftain's house at the far end of the village. There was no one else around, anywhere.

I finally spotted Mazar sitting under a tree, and joined him. After sitting there with him for a few minutes, I noticed that some of the other villagers came out of their houses and went about on the dirt street that cut through the center of town, like any other day.

Mazar didn't say, but I got the feeling that there was some tension between the chemists and the people of Sra Kala, when they came back to continue the synthesis, the townspeople disappeared again.

Definitely some tension there.

They put the cooled cooking pots on the Bunsen burners for about thirty minutes, and poured the heated solution through a cheese cloth filter.

The solid sludge-like material that stuck to the filter was rinsed into an empty drum that was then filled with more hot water; the solution was filtered several more times.

Finally the cheese cloth itself was placed in a portable laundry press to squeeze out any of the remaining pulp; it then went into to the sludge drum. Then they dropped a bunch of sodium carbonate powder into the drum, and covered it until it stopped fizzing.

After rinsing and filtering the whole mix a few more times, and steaming off any leftover water, they poured it, still sludge-like, into a few rectangular baking pans where they continued kneading it with steel paint stirrers until dry enough to let the air do the rest. That was it—kinda looked like lumpy brown sugar.

The final weight came in at just over sixty-five kilos.

"I'm told there is two-hundred-fifty kilos of raw opium remaining in the fields," said Hamman.

"I think so," I answered, "Khatol said she scored the pods yesterday, I'll help them collect it tomorrow morning."

"I'm sure it will take more than two days to collect two-hundred-fifty kilos," he said, "please bring it to me as soon as soon as you have cooked it."

He turned to go back to his father's house for the night.

I went back to my hooch for the night. Mazar brought me a few pieces of chicken and a pot of tea for dinner.

"I have a few questions Mazar, what's up between the chemists and the people of Sra Kala?"

"Pashtuns are generally very conservative, they do not approve of them."

"Next question, why didn't the chemists go to the mosque, or do the Salaat at all today? Aren't they Muslim too?"

"They have been excommunicated and are banned from the Mosque, the Imam does not approve of their chosen profession either."

"What do you mean?"

"Well, heroin is expressly forbidden by Islam, like alcohol and every other intoxicant, it is haram. They might not use it, I don't know if they do or not, but either way, they make It."

"What about Khatol," I said, "and the other farmers? I've seen them go to the Mosque, or pray in the fields. They grow poppies don't they? Isn't that a double standard?"

"No, not to the townspeople," he answered, "Khatol and the others are just that, farmers. In Pashtun society, farming and soldiering are the two most honorable professions. So they grow poppies. Most people here feel that they are just plants after all, they are natural, Allah has provided them.

"And what is that phrase from the west, 'God helps those who help themselves,' the mujahideen sell the poppies to finance the war with the Soviets, the chemists are necessary, if they were not, they surely would have been killed by now, most likely by their own fathers. The townspeople believe that Hamman and his cousins take something natural, something made by Allah, and they adulterate it. I myself do not necessarily agree with this thinking."

Mazar left me to eat my chicken and drink my tea in silence.

17

Later that night, I woke up hearing Toshi come in. He'd sustained a slight injury during an ambush; a timed explosive detonated early, leaving him with a shoulder full of shrapnel.

"It is not bad," he said, "just a few stitches, but I may have to go a few days without swinging a sword."

After having killed several soldiers with the sword or bow, I don't think he wanted to go back to using a rifle; there was no Honor in it.

"Mahmoud sent me back here to rest my shoulder. He and the others are still in Jalalabad, they will return in a few days."

"I have to get up early to help finish with the harvest." I said as I was headed back towards my bed.

Passing his gear in the corner, I noticed that there were several notches carved on his quiver, and on his scabbard.

Before the sun came up, I was knocking on Khatol's front door; it was pretty windy that morning. I had dropped off the processed heroin the night before in two large plastic garbage bags, and she had already begun to separate it into sixty-five one kilogram bricks, wrapping each in heavy black plastic visqueen sheeting and duct taping the corners.

Mazar had gone back to Peshawar the night before, but between some crude sign language and the few Pashto words I'd picked up in the last few months, I was confident that communicating wouldn't be a problem.

Khatol said that she wanted to finish wrapping the product, and would join us later. She pointed me to three other houses where the women, who'd performed the collection before, lived.

They came out and climbed into the wagon I was driving. There were six of them, and I hadn't noticed before, but they were all 'marrying age,' and a few were fairly young, but none of them was wearing a burka.

A group of armed men, their husbands or brothers I figured, followed me on horseback to the poppy fields.

Toshi woke with a start; the wind was howling through the trees, and the sun was shining in the window. His shoulder was sore, but that wasn't what had awakened him; he had a strange feeling: it was too quiet.

He dressed quickly, grabbed his swords and bow, and went out into the woods behind the house. He climbed a tree so that he could see what was going on in the valley.

Shortly he saw three Russian soldiers emerge from the forest opposite the village. For them to approach an Afghan village so boldly, he knew that they must have been watching for sometime to be sure that it was empty before making a move. They went to the front door of Khatol's house.

Of all of the houses in Sra Kala, it is strange that they would choose the smallest, unless they had some prior knowledge.

Khatol had finished wrapping the heroin, and the sixty-five bricks were in a large green military duffel that lay by the door.

Just as she was preparing to go help with the collection and extraction of the remaining opium, her fifteen-year-old granddaughter came over for a visit. They were cleaning the dishes and stacking them on the table in the main room, when the Russians kicked down the door.

The two women shrieked in terror as the soldiers rushed in.

Doski saw the green duffel lying by the door, and knowing what was inside, picked it up.

"I'll be back with the Krokodil in a few minutes," he called to his comrades, Yuri and Vladimir, as he ran out the door.

They both grunted a response, turned back and went to get the little Afghan girl. Yuri knew that since Vladimir was bigger than him, he would go first.

Vladimir, with one hand outstretched to grab her, and the other hand holding his rifle by the pistol grip, caught and dragged her, kicking and screaming into the back room and closed the door behind him.

Yuri hoped Vladimir wouldn't be too long, but knew he would take his time.

The girl was screaming.

"Do not kill her Vladimir!" demanded Yuri.

Vladimir did not respond to him, and the girl kept screaming and thrashing about.

Yuri realized that he would have to entertain himself for the time being. I'll antagonize the old bitch, he thought.

He began cursing at her, and pushing her away from the door to the backroom. When she started clawing at him wildly, uselessly fighting with everything left in her eighty-five-year-old body to go to her granddaughter's aid, he laughed and spit on her.

Finally he pushed her to the ground, and jumped up onto the table. He slung his rifle over his shoulder, and undid his belt buckle, dropping his pants to his knees.

In the backroom, Vladimir was impressed because the girl was still fighting him. He had slapped her to the floor several times, and had even punched her once or twice, but still she fought. She fights with the courage of a people who will not be broken, he thought.

Then he pulled out a telescoping baton, and extended it.

Crack! The steel baton bounced off the top of her head and the girl collapsed to the floor. The hulking Soviet then lowered his pants to expose his erection, reached down to remove her underpants, and commenced to rape her.

The Afghans had learned to always have a back door, just in case an escape was necessary. And Toshi had already moved into position behind and above Vladimir where there was a loft in the ceiling.

With his short sword drawn, he leaped down while swinging it, and with his full weight on the To, cut the big Russian's head and left shoulder off, the half of his torso with the head attached fell one way, and the other half fell the other way. A torrent of blood splashed the girl, who was still unconscious.

Hearing the thud, Yuri cried out,

"Damn you Vladimir! I said don't kill her!"

The old woman was still down on the floor, and Yuri was still on the table with his pants down at his knees.

"Watch this, you old bitch!" he said.

He squatted over the stack of newly cleaned dishes, pulled down his thermal underwear, and started shitting on the dishes.

Khatol still couldn't get up, but when she saw what he was doing, anger like Yuri had never seen before crossed her face.

Toshi pushed the door open slightly so he could see out, the table was less than two meters in front of the door, and Yuri was facing the other way.

Khatol could see Toshi, but she kept her glare on the Russian.

Once he had crept within pouncing distance, he lunged.

Grabbing for his rifle's pistol grip, Yuri spun around in time to see Toshi cut his right leg off at the knee; he fell to the floor with the stack of dishes.

Doski had been coming back to get Yuri and Vladimir when he heard the crash, and he flung the door open. Toshi instantly threw the four pointed shuriken, but the startled Soviet slammed the door shut, and ran back to the waiting Hind.

Toshi wondered how he could've missed the sound of an approaching helicopter.

Khatol was up and had Yuri by the hair. She was suddenly much stronger than before, cursing at him and grinding his face into her soiled plate.

She shattered the plate across his forehead and began cutting his nose off with shards of the shattered porcelain. Then his ears, his lips, and finally she cut his tongue out, and let him fall to the floor on his back to drown in his own blood.

Toshi was slightly repulsed by the old woman's brutality, but knew there was no time to protest.

"Chatak—Mekh Dara!!!" he shouted, hoping she would understand him.

She did, and he bent down to scoop up her still dazed granddaughter as they scrambled out the back door and down into the creek behind the row of thatch roofed houses.

A brief second after they'd reached safety, Khatol's house was obliterated by a rocket blast from the airborne Hind. They were showered with burning splinters and broken glass.

Once he set the young girl down against a tree, Toshi started back down the row of houses for the bow and quiver he'd left hanging in a tree behind the house he shared with Randall.

The Hind had begun targeting each house down the line, luckily much of Sra Kala was empty; most of the town's residents were busy in the fields planting next year's crops.

There squeezing goo from the poppies, I thought for sure I heard the main rotor whir of a big helicopter, but told myself that it was just the wind. When the first shot rang out however, I stopped and looked towards the town.

Moments later an explosion sounded and a thick cloud of smoke rose into the air, right over the same spot.

I rushed to the wagon. Another explosion echoed through the valley, and another, and another. Both horses were tugging at their reins. I turned to reach for the RPG-7 lying in the wagon bed, when I noticed that the Pashtun farmers who didn't trust me alone with their women earlier, were now my back up.

As I was racing towards the center of the village in the wagon, I finally saw what was responsible for the explosions, it was a Hind.

"Oh shit!!" I gasped.

I grabbed the RPG off the bench seat, and tried to aim it with one hand, and drive the horses with the other.

I knew it would take some practice before I'd be able to make a 'magic shot' like that one Jafir and Khaleed brought down their Hind with, but thought maybe I could distract it away from flattening the village further, at least temporarily.

I was just out of the forest between Sra Kala and its farmland, where the end of the wooded path opens onto the town's main street.

I was looking through the peephole viewfinder on the RPG, and just as I fired the weapon, I heard a burst a fire from my left.

I knew that I'd fallen into a trap. In a flash, the horses were riddled with bullets, and the wagon was going over on its right side. But it didn't stop on its side, it went on over, trapping me underneath.

There was a little space between the ground and the sides of the wagon bed where I could see that I'd missed the Hind.

That's when I saw what had shot the wagon out from under me. I was surprised because I hadn't seen one in about thirteen years; It was an MI-1 Hare, a little three seat chopper; the NVA used them to gather reconnaissance and to ferry officers from Hanoi to points in the field.

They were fast, quiet, and easy to fly. They didn't have much armor on them, and weapons systems were usually limited to a pilot aimed machinegun, but the Hare could definitely kick some ass. This one had some kind of Vulcan type Gatling gun fixed under its fuselage.

I watched the Hare fly to within a few meters of my overturned wagon, touch down, and drop off a commando armed with a Shorty AK. He's here to finish me off.

Alright, I thought, you won't get me without a fight. I still had one RPG left, and figured that even trapped down here I would be able to take one shot.

But I guess he thought I was already dead, because he walked on by. I couldn't see where he was going, but I could hear that little AK going off and I heard screaming.

Oh shit, he's in the hospital!!

I was looking for a way to get out from under my trappings, when Toshi came out of nowhere.

"Jack? Are you ok?"

"I'm ok, but my legs are pinched underneath."

"We have to hurry Jack! The helicopters…"

I saw him waving his hands under the far end of the wagon, and I understood that he meant to lift it high enough for me to squeeze out. He was much stronger than I ever would've guessed.

Afterwards he disappeared back into the trees

behind the now leveled row of houses.

"I've got to get my bow…"

I moved around to the front side of the hospital tent, and could still hear the Soviet commando ransacking the place.

The Hind and the Hare were still at the other end of the village compound.

Suddenly, Zmarak ran out of the tent, but didn't see me. He was watching the helicopters; the Hind was out of rockets, but one of the soldiers onboard was leaning out the window port firing an RPG, and the Hare was coming back towards the hospital. He made a beeline for the edge of the forest.

"Zmarak, don't run in a Straight Line!" I yelled, wishing I knew how to say zigzag in Pashto.

The commando came out with his gun ready and pointed at the little boy's back. And I started running at him.

"No, Zmarak, Juke!" I shouted, "Kin-Shay! Zigzag! Zmara—"

Two short bursts from the Soviet's machine gun threw the boy's arms in the air, a third picked up his little body, and it was over.

I hit that motherfucker flat out on a full speed run. Knocked him right fucking down, put my knees down on his shoulder blades, and grabbed the top of his head and started pounding his face into the ground.

"Piece of fucking shit! Gonna' shoot a little boy in the back?!"

I reached down to my belt with my left hand and unsnapped my SOG Bowie, pulled it out and raised it up to eye level.

Then while still clutching the top clump of the Soviet's hair, I scraped the edge of the knife along his hairline, until I was peeling-off his scalp, and he was crying like a little girl.

I held it up to the Hare pilot who was now flying straight at me.

"Here comes your comrade," I said to the sobbing commando.

"What's he gonna' do now?" I asked playfully.

He may not have even understood English, but it didn't matter anyway.

"I bet I know what he's gonna' do..."

Noticing that he was wearing a fairly heavy duty flak jacket, I threw down his hair flap, and got off of his back. And just as the pilot started shooting, I pulled him up in front of me by the top of his jacket. He saw what was going to happen, and screamed.

"Nyet! Nyet!"

And when the 7.6 mm rounds tore into his chest, his body tightened up, and he screamed once more; then he went limp and quiet.

I was a little concerned about the bullets going through him into me, but none did; a split second later, miraculously, the Hare exploded!

Da svidanyia comrades...

Toshi had been trying to get back to his longbow for several minutes after Khatol's house exploded. But each time he started, the Hind would begin another attack too close to permit an attempt.

Just then the gunship stopped firing, and Toshi noticed that the rocket pods, hanging below its stubby wings, were empty.

Taking advantage of this sudden lull in the fight, he again made a break for the weapon.

This time he stopped short because he noticed, across the courtyard, a small helicopter hovering by the entrance of the town center, it was sitting ready in ambush position.

Taking care not to leave the cover of the forest, he moved closer to the clearing in hopes of hearing something, anything that would clue him in to what the little chopper was waiting for.

At first Toshi couldn't hear anything from the path, then the sound of thundering hooves reached him, and he knew there were charging horses coming. He also knew that he would not be able to warn the riders of the impending attack.

Seconds later, the wagon carrying Jack Randall came galloping into view. Just as the helicopter's Gatling gun erupted, Randall's RPG went off.

The Hind had obviously been the target, but the sudden burst of fire had apparently startled him and the shot missed completely.

The horses were cut down immediately and the wagon was sent sliding off the road, only to flip over and come to rest upside down.

Toshi rushed to the overturned wagon to see if

Jack was hurt.

"Jack, Jack, can you hear me? Can you move?"

Hearing some reassuring sounds from underneath, he then began to call him over to its corner, where there was a small gap between the ground and the wagon bed's edge.

With all of his strength, he was able to lift the wagon just enough that Randall could get out from under it. Seeing that Jack was out, and had not been shot, Toshi made his way back into the woods, and headed straight for his bow and quiver.

By the time he reached his weapons, a soldier in the Hind had begun firing an RPG-7 from the window port. The RPG was certainly not as powerful as the 80 mm unguided rockets, but with the soldier aiming each shot, it was still quite destructive.

Toshi recognized the soldier leaning out of the Hind as the same one who had barely evaded his shuriken attack back at Khatol's; Doski, he remembered the others calling him.

While Doski was firing in the opposite direction, he knocked an arrow and stepped out of the woods. Toshi raised the bow, just like when he was giving his demonstration of Kyudo to the children of Sra Kala, and he lowered it to his eyebrow, while simultaneously drawing the bow into a Kai-full draw.

While holding the shot momentarily to concentrate on his breathing, he saw Doski turn his head towards him and he knew that he'd been seen.

Quickly, Doski reloaded the RPG-7 and turned, leaned out the window and took direct aim at Toshi.

But he didn't rush, as if performing a well rehearsed dance step, Toshi calmly released the willow leaf tipped Ya. Seconds later, in a blur, Doski jerked his head back, stood up straight and spun to his right, the RPG launched.

The last command that Doski's brain sent down through his spinal cord to his trigger finger was temporarily interrupted, and he knew that something had hit him, Suddenly his throat burned, he could taste blood, and a great alarm bell went off in his head.

He realized he was falling backwards and, as if helplessly watching from the other side of the helicopter's cargo bay, saw himself raising the unfired RPG until it was pointing across the town center at the Hare.

Before he blacked out his brain sent that final command through, and his finger twitched against the trigger of the rocket propelled grenade launcher.

Doski was dead before he hit the floor of the Hind, the last RPG he fired traveled almost three hundred meters, and hit the little helo in the center of the pilot's canopy door.

The Hind may be known as 'a flying tank,' but the Hare is more like a flying VW Bug.

With his eyes fixed on Randall, the Hare pilot never saw it coming.

When the Hind pilot saw the Hare explode,

he immediately turned the big gunship around and flew back to the base in Mehtar Lam where he knew he would be in deep shit: they had taken the two helicopters without permission from the senior commander.

18

After the Hind left, the people of Sra Kala returned from the fields and assessed the damage done to their village.

About nine of the houses were completely destroyed, three others were badly damaged. A total of ten people, including five inside the hospital, still in their beds, and Zmarak, were killed; most of the livestock was also killed.

The next morning, Mahmoud and the others returned. They had been observing Jalalabad Air Base from atop a nearby mountain, when Khaleed noticed the black smoke coming from Sra Kala. They abandoned their ambush, and hightailed it back to investigate.

Even though I knew Mahmoud didn't blame me for the attack, I felt responsible. It wasn't a sanctioned military offense, it was just a couple of renegade Soviets: they came for the dope.

They got it too, knew right where to look for it; I guess there was a spy in Sra Kala after all.

The Hind pilot probably wouldn't be in a rush to explain to his superiors, why he and five other guys took the two helicopters, without permission, for a spin, so I doubted if another patrol was coming.

When I explained to Mahmoud what happened, and that only two helicopters had attacked, he agreed with me. He asked which direction the Hind flew off in.

"Just a little west of due-north," I answered him.

"Bagram Air Base is one hundred ninety kilometers north-west. Jalalabad Air Base is also north-west, but only forty five kilometers away. There is another, a much-smaller base, with much-less security—a base where soldiers would have more access to take a few helicopters for an unauthorized mission. It is only ninety five kilometers away, and as you say, 'a little west of due-north,' it is called Mehtar Lam Outpost. It houses one hundred soldiers, give or take."

It wasn't revenge I was after; I had to get that heroin back!

After planting it, and harvesting it, and processing it, I wasn't about to let it go that easy, I was going to go get it. I didn't want to ask Mahmoud for any help, taking care of the dope was my deal.

But I hoped Toshi would go with me.

"I will go," he said without me even asking.

Quickly, I grabbed two duffel kit bags of weapons. And Toshi brought his stuff too; sword and bow and whatnot. I did ask Mahmoud to give us a ride closer to the base.

Jafir took us in one of the pick-up trucks that Toshi had given Mahmoud, and he dropped us off about thirty kilometers from the base.

"Do you want me to wait for you?"

"No," I said, "you should get back, Mahmoud needs your help."

Before he drove off, he gave Toshi one of the radios.

"We will monitor channel thirty-seven, if you need anything. But don't let any vital information go out over the line..."

We were just outside the wire when the sun went down. Toshi wanted to go over the plan, and get the equipment ready.

Wouldn't you know it; in the hurry I had grabbed the wrong bag. Instead of the one with the C-4 and detonators, I grabbed the one with a tent, about twenty-five meters of fishing line, a roll of duct tape, five M-80s, two packages of Black Cat firecrackers, two Bic lighters, and a pair of night vision goggles. Not sure what I had fireworks for.

"We'll need to get closer to see before I figure out what to do," I said, probably more for myself than for Toshi.

I gave the night goggles to Toshi, along with the duct tape, the Bic lighter, and a few of the M-80s. I took three metal tent spikes, the fishing line, my shotgun, a utility knife, a Leatherman tool, an M-18 smoke grenade, and an M-67 fragmentation grenade, the other lighter and the Black Cats.

Toshi was a real bad-ass, we didn't know who, what, or how many, we were going up against, and all he was bringing was his sword, a knife, his bow, and a quiver of arrows.

After we were set, we advanced the final fifteen hundred meters to the field-base. We found a hide among some scrub trees at a point just beyond the barbwire fenced perimeter of the base, and watched for a while.

There were two guard towers, one on either end of the encampment, with three barrack quonsets and a metal warehouse/hangar in the middle.

There were also five helicopter pads out beyond the towers, Hinds were on three of them; the other two were empty.

I guess it made sense to separate the fly-zone and the towers. But what about security for the he-licopters? As I continued to scan, I could see there were three fighting-holes in front of the hangar, and there was a cherry walking around in one of them.

"Listen up dumb-shits!" the words from my DI at basic came back to me, "don't ever openly smoke cigarettes in your holes at night...the enemy will spot you from way off and you'll be dead in the morning."

These guys must not have been told that.

The helicopters were about twenty meters apart from each other, about thirty meters away from the hangar and about one hundred meters from the first hole. There was a shallow ditch running around the base, about fifteen meters from the helicopters.

"I'm going to disable two of those helicopters," I said. "I'll need you to make some diversion for me…keep an eye on me with the night glasses, and tape a few of the M-80s to your arrows, when I give you the thumbs-up, light 'em and shoot 'em, at the barracks there on the right. While everyone is looking the other way, I'll get in close to those Hinds, and see what I can rig. I'm betting the heroin is in that hangar. I'll get in, get it, and fly us out of here in that third Hind."

Toshi looked at me.

"Jack, is that realistic? Do you really think you can do that?"

"Sure I can do that; here you're ready to go up against, maybe sixty guys or more, with a sword and a bow and arrows…I'm just gonna' steal a helicopter."

He stopped and looked at me.

"No Jack, I mean, can you fly a helicopter?"

"Oh yeah! I flew helicopters in Vietnam."

Well, I did about two weeks helicopter training before I left the States, part of Ranger training, but I only flew in Vietnam three or four times, thirteen years ago. But I also spent a few years flying from Kowloon to Macau, a few times a month, in a little Bell single engine chopper.

"After your diversion, just wait here, or maybe even start walking back to Sra Kala. If all goes as planned, I'll pick you up in that Hind over there shortly," I pointed off to the left. "If it doesn't go as planned, well you know...you don't want to get captured by these guys."

As I crept closer to the first Hind, I noticed a few strange little bushes coming out of the ground.

When I ran a closer inspection of the bush nearest me, I could tell right away that it wasn't a bush at all. It was a piece of plastic netting covering something, a light maybe? Carefully, I felt around the base of the thing, clawing through the dirt behind it with my index finger, looking for a wire.

When I found it, it kinda' felt like a power cord. But no, it was familiar to me, I just couldn't place it. Then it hit me, and suddenly I felt very stupid, because I knew I was on the wrong end of the Soviet version of the Claymore.

Claymores have three modes of detonation: Command Detonation—this means that the soldier using the weapon has to trigger it, Victim Detonation—this means it is rigged with a tripwire, and Time Delay—in this mode a timer is used to activate detonation.

I couldn't remember what to do next, but some clarity came to me after a minute.

"If it had been outfitted with a tripwire, it would have already vaporized me," I whispered to myself.

I relaxed a little. Then I saw that there were about four or five of these Russian Claymores clustered together every fifteen or so meters, facing away from the helicopters.

Of course! The mines are the security for the helicopters!

I could also reasonably assume that the mines, in each of these clusters, were daisy-chained together, so that one trigger mechanism would detonate all of the mines, either simultaneously or consecutively.

I remembered the lesson Sergeant Honcho gave us in Vietnam on Claymore placement.

"You have to be careful where you place 'em," he said, "be sure you can see 'em at all times. If you put 'em where you can't see 'em, the enemy can dig 'em up and turn 'em around, so when you trigger 'em, they'll blow your stupid ass to pieces."

I gave Toshi the closed-fist signal, hoping he would understand that I needed some time. With my knife I dug a pit around the mine, just like I was transplanting a cactus. When it was free, I turned it around to face the Hind and packed in the loose-dirt. I quickly turned the other four mines in the cluster similarly. Hinds are pretty tough, but having five Claymores exploded right into it...

There was another Hind next to the right side

of the ditch, with another cluster of mines on the other side of that. But I didn't want to leave the cover of the ditch long enough to dig up the mines.

I had something else in mind; I had that pineapple grenade, the fishing line and a tent spike. Now of course a hand grenade wouldn't even scratch its armor, but if it was in the engine compartment when it detonated, it would cause a major malfunction.

I tied one end of the fishing line to the grenade's pull-ring, and the other to one of the tent spikes that I'd pounded into the side of the ditch with the butt of my hammer-ended utility knife. And with the needle-nose pliers on the Leatherman tool, I straightened out the grenade's safety-pin. I was ready to go.

I needed that distraction to get everyone looking the other way first. Toshi was on it. He'd been watching me, and on my signal, he loosed about three arrows, with lit M-80s taped to them.

The arrows stuck in the roof of the barracks, and the M-80s made a lot of noise, almost like a mini artillery strike.

I wasted no time, was out of that ditch and back behind that helicopter in a flash, carefully paying-out the fishing line as I ran.

I found the engine access door, popped it open, put the fragger in there, and closed it on the line; it was pretty taut, and I doubted if the Hind would even get off the ground before the pin was pulled.

I still had the smoker on my belt. Crouching

behind the helicopter, I took a quick look at the third Hind; it was only thirty meters away, but kind of out in the open; I didn't think I'd be able to get over to it, but the cargo door was half-open, and there was something laying on the floor of the gunship.

Just then, I heard the sound of a helicopter engine starting up.

I turned around and saw, the MI-24's cousin, the MI-8 Hip, taking off from back where Toshi was hiding; I knew they'd probably caught him.

I took advantage of the second, unplanned, diversion, and darted over to the third Hind, ducked behind it, out of the line-of-site of the fighting-holes.

Peering through the door's window into the cargo area, I saw that it was a body—the soldier that Toshi had killed with his incredible bow shot.

I needed one more diversion, to get those guys in the hole to detonate those Claymores I'd turned around.

I found a baseball sized rock on the ground, wrapped a string of firecrackers around it, lit the fuse and threw it towards the fence I came over.

The soldiers set off the Claymores. They were daisy-chained together; all five of them ripped into the Hind. It didn't explode, but it wasn't going anyplace too soon.

Before they realized what had happened, I Hail-Mary'd the smoker as far as I could towards that first hole.

It had to be over one hundred fifty meters, so I doubt if it went in, but I just needed a temporary curtain. Soon, clouds of white smoke billowed forth.

I climbed into the cargo-bay, and over the dead guy, noticing that his throat was all torn open. Then I squeezed through the narrow passageway that led to the flight deck, and sat in the rear tandem seat.

Looking over the mechanical control panel, I quickly found the four main flight controls, common to all helicopters: collective, cyclic, the rudders, and the throttle. The biggest difference in the controls was the throttle: in a single engine helicopter the throttle is a motorcycle-style twist grip on the end of the collective lever, but on a twin-engine helicopter, like the Hind, the throttle is a governor unit with two power levers.

Before coming to Afghanistan, Pik took me over to the Kowloon Municipal Airport to meet a Russian pilot friend of his.

Anatoly Straichausky was an ex-Soviet pilot; he'd been stationed in East Berlin when he defected to the Germans. He hadn't defected with a Hind or anything like that, but the KGB, Russian Secret Police, wanted him dead anyway, so he was on the lamb for a while, that's how he ended up in Hong Kong.

Anatoly was a hulk of a man with jet-black hair and a cratered face. He worked at KMA as a helicopter mechanic.

"Oh yes," he said with a thick Russian accent,

"the Mil MI-24, we called them flying tanks, be-cause they are so un-maneuverable, or Krokodils because they look prehistoric. Very fast, but they don't hover well. It is big and heavy, and the stubby little wings block the rotor downwash needed for hovering. Without those wings though, it wouldn't be able to get off the ground. When fully loaded with weapons they can't lift-off from a standstill, but need a rolling start."

He had me look at some cockpit schematics, and gave me a few hints about flying one.

"Watch out for sharp turns at high speeds," he said, "especially if you're in a dive, don't try to pull-up too fast. The fuselage to tail section has a problem with flexing and the main rotor can hit the tail boom, causing the thing to crash. But also, remember that the tail rotor is very fragile, the Kro-kodil's Achilles' heel."

As I got the engines going, I started taking small-arms fire from the hangar. I squeezed the trigger on the stick, and silenced 'em with a blast from the chain-gun. Then I eased the big machine into a slight roll, increased the collective pitch, and lifted off.

I pushed the cyclic forward to bring the nose down and give the Bird a little more forward mo-tion, and folded the tricycle-style landing gear, pulled the cyclic back to neutral, and pushed the left pedal down; the tail spun to the right. Then I let up on the left pedal and pushed down the right to bring the tail back to center.

After my little warm-up to get familiar with flying the Hind, I went after the Hip.

I saw a flight crew running towards the Hind I'd booby-trapped, but didn't even try to stop them from getting in it. I knew they wouldn't get far.

The sun was just coming up behind me, and I could barely see the transport chopper way far ahead of me.

Though maneuvering the Hind was painfully slow, just like Anatoly said it would be, if you kept it in a straight line, it hauled-ass.

I was cruising at two hundred forty kilometers per hour, making some gains on the other helicopter, but it was still in the lead by more than twenty five kilometers.

Of course I didn't know for sure, but I hoped Toshi was on board, and that Pik's dope was too. Then I remembered about Bagram Air Base being in this direction, and hoped they weren't going there.

A few minutes later, on the horizon, to my right, I saw two big cargo looking planes heading north, flying low like they just took off.

"There's the airbase," I said out loud, and turned a hair south; the Hip's pilot made a slight turn south as well.

19

As the frightened Soviet helicopter pilot touched down on the pad at the Mehtar Lam Outpost, thoughts ran through his head—what happened? What am I going to do? But nothing came to his mind. And then he remembered Major Rasullah, the DRA commander who acted as deputy to Red Army General Chezkovich.

Normally, the Communist Afghans were looked down on—never respected, never trusted, whether or not they had higher rank. But this time, Stepkavic would revere him; he knew that Rasullah was his only hope of escaping the Siberian Gulag or worse.

Months ago, rumors began spreading about soldiers being killed by ninjas, and Major Rasullah was most interested. Just exactly why, Stepkavic wasn't sure. But maybe since he had witnessed one of the ninjas kill his comrade—indirectly destroying the Hare, maybe the DRA Major would help him.

He quickly left the Hind-D and ran into the hangar hoping to find Rasullah in his office.

"Excuse me," he said to the office-clerk, "I'm looking for Major Rasullah."

"He is around back, with the duhki prisoners."

Behind the hangar was a small ten meter square, fenced in with barbed wire, and Rasullah was there getting his daily workout; he was surrounded by five prisoners armed with Mongol cavalry swords.

"If you can overcome me," he offered them a deal–speaking in Afghan Farsi, "then you are free to go."

The three armed guards standing by made the sincerity of his offer seem doubtful, but one last chance to kill an infidel communist was enough incentive to goad these men into a fight.

Ever since examining the bodies of the five Russians back in February, he'd become so excited about facing a Samurai that he had started practicing with a katana. He liked its feel; it was so much lighter than the sword of his ancestors.

Rasullah was a fearsome opponent, even without a rifle, as these prisoners would learn.

Two prisoners attacked from the front and rear; simultaneously charging with swords raised over their heads.

He immediately went low, spun around one hundred eighty degrees, and swiped his sword across the advancing prisoner's midsection, and without waiting for the man's intestines to spill out, completed the circle—while returning to his full height, and with both hands on his sword's handle, drove its blade through the other man's chest.

The three remaining insurgents quickly realized that the "blind rush" didn't make for a very effective strategy. They still had the major surrounded though, and began slowly closing in on him with swords out front.

Rasullah sized up his opponents. The two in front were the more formidable of the three. He could tell by the way they'd cleared their faces of all emotion, and by the way they held their swords with both hands, that they were seasoned warriors. He glanced over his shoulder every few seconds.

The prisoner behind him was just a boy barely out of his teens, and he could see fear in his eyes. He also noted that the boy was holding his sword with only one hand—his right hand.

Slowly he took a step backwards, closing the distance between him and the boy, and turned sideways so his left side was now facing the two warriors.

He was still focusing the majority of his attention on them, but looked back one last time. Then he imperceptibly shifted his weight to his right leg, and gave the older two insurgents a slight smile, as if to say: Watch this.

He spun around, kicking-out with his left leg, catching the end of the boy's blade on its side with the heel of his boot. The kick didn't knock the sword from his one hand grip, but it did push it out to his side, leaving him exposed to a frontal attack.

Rasullah stepped in quickly, and with one hand on the back of his blade, made a deep slash down across his upper torso–from the left-side of his throat to the top of his pelvis.

The young insurgent fell on his back, and fighting to breathe, continued to aspirate blood for several minutes. Ignoring the sound, Rasullah turned to face the others.

"Show some mercy! you coward…" said one of the fighters.

Reluctantly, he called one of the guards and pointed.

"Yussuf, shoot him in the head."

The Kalashnikov rang out, and the gurgling stopped.

His remaining opponents seemed unsettled by the gunshot; perhaps they've realized that today is their last, he thought.

The two circled around him to attack from both sides, and closed in until both were less than three meters away from him.

The major quickly reevaluated the situation; the insurgent on the right seems less sure of himself, he thought.

While smiling at the man on his left, Rasullah lunged, sword first, towards the other.

Caught off guard, the insurgent tried to back up, but lost his footing on a large smooth rock, and fell backwards.

Corporal Stepkavic walked out the back door of the hangar in time to see Major Rasullah decapitate the duhki.

"You dirty Hazara coward!" the final prisoner yelled, throwing down his sword. "Fight me without that sword!"

Rasullah happily complied; he re-sheathed his sword and laid it on the ground. The two squared off, and though the insurgent was both taller and heavier than him, he was not worried.

The bearded insurgent charged in to grapple him. But Rasullah evaded him easily. They were now standing very close to each other, and neither of them could see any fear in the other man's eyes. When he saw the man snarl and clench his fists, the Major knew another charge was coming.

This time he just stepped to his left, and threw a stiff uppercut that connected the heel of his right hand with the charging prisoner's septum—driving his nose bone into his brain, thus ending the fight.

Yussuf and the two other DRA guards had seen similar displays from Major Rasullah in the past.

They had become quite bored with them, but they knew it was a good idea to applaud loudly.

20

Stepkavic walked to the edge of the enclosure, he noted that Major Rasullah wasn't even breathing heavy after facing the five insurgents.

He saluted the senior officer. "Sir, I must speak to you privately...immediately..."

Rasullah was slightly annoyed by the young man's insistence, but the large satchel he was carrying aroused his curiosity, and the fact that the Red Army officer saluted him was also very enticing.

He returned the Corporal's salute, and motioned for him to follow.

"Yussuf!" he barked, "get someone to cleanup this mess, will you!"

Stepkavic thought about what he would say as they walked through the hangar and down the hallway to the offices.

"I've just come from a small village in Nangar-har province," he started, "and I think I have evidence of the ninja operating with the mujahideen."

The major was immediately interested.

"Please excuse us, Sergeant," he said to the clerk.

Stepkavic watched as the man quickly left the room, closing the door behind him.

"Please go on Corporal Stepkavic," said Rasullah, switching to Russian.

Stepkavic turned to face him. "I have a problem Major…"

He gave the full report of all that had happened, including the part where he and five others had taken the two helicopters, unauthorized, to steal ninety kilos of heroin from the insurgents.

When Rasullah asked to see the body of Corporal Doski, Stepkavic took him out to the helicopter and showed him.

He watched in horror as the Major carelessly pulled the arrow out of Doski's throat, and wiped the arrowhead off on the dead man's shirt.

A small group of soldiers, mostly Soviets, had begun to gather curiously around the helicopter. But the DRA Major only eyed them contemptuously.

"This helicopter is off-limits," he said to them, "no one is to come near it."

Walking away he noticed that none of the Soviets were listening to him.

"That is a direct order from General Chezkovich!" shouted Rasullah, "I am authorized to shoot violators," he added angrily.

At that the soldiers moved away from the helicopter, and he turned to go back to his office. "Come with me Stepkavic."

Back at his desk, he studied the arrowhead closely, as if reading it like a book. When he finished he showed it to the Corporal.

"This is a Yanagi-bu." He held the slim four-sided arrowhead between his thumb and index finger.

"It is shaped like the Willow leaf, and has several engravings on it. These," he pointed to two characters on the backside of it, "represent the owner's Ancestral-Clan Name, I believe the name is Ushido Hitoshi."

He turned it over to reveal another engraving, having five characters.

"These represent a Haiku, Japanese poetry, it reads: Unknown as a Ghost—Swift and ever so silent—From the sky it comes.

"Quaint, unimaginative dribble. Don't you think?" Rasullah looked up, shrugging.

"What does it mean sir?"

"You aren't very smart, are you Stepkavic?" he said, rolling his eyes.

"No sir, I guess not," the young Corporal answered.

"It refers to death, swift and silent death, at the hands of the dukhis-ghost insurgents."

With that Rasullah fell quiet, and just stared at the miniature spear head for what seemed like hours to Stepkavic; he finally broke the silence

"Now you must tell me everything you remember about this ninja. Was it only one man? Was the bow his only weapon? How many others did you see him kill?

Besides Doski, and the one in the Hare? That amount of heroin, ninety kilos, must certainly be worth a small fortune; perhaps he will come and try to get it back."

"Sir," Stepkavic hesitantly interrupted, "I weighed the satchel of heroin, to be sure of the amount, and it is only sixty-five kilos."

Rasullah did not reply, but only stared expectantly.

The Corporal talked for hours, while Major Rasullah just listened; asking additional questions frequently.

"I will help you Corporal Stepkavic, and you will help me; quid pro quo."

Unsure what that meant, the Soviet just nodded.

"General Chezkovich is in Kabul, he will be there for a few days and I am in charge of this camp until he returns. I will send the other Soviets to Bagram for supplies. You must convince them to go, and then we–you, me, and my DRA Garrison–will lay a trap for this ninja. You said he fought alone, there will be thirty-nine heavily armed soldiers waiting for him when he gets here; this is what we will do…"

Stepkavic was able to convince the other Soviets to go, though they didn't really need the supplies; he reminded them that the prostitutes from Turkestan would be there tonight, and that was all it took. All thirty-five Soviets loaded into five KAMaz trucks and headed west on the dirt road for the seventy kilometer ride to Bagram. He made sure they knew that it was all right for them to spend the night, and return tomorrow, he even gave them a forged letter from General Chezkovich authorizing their mission.

Rasullah ordered fifteen of the remaining thirty-nine Afghan soldiers to accompany him to the tree line, just beyond the base's perimeter; Stepkavic would fly them in an Mi-8 Hip, and once there they would camouflage the transport helicopter and wait.

The sun had gone down an hour ago. Through the Pine forest they were able to see the base, but hadn't seen anything happening yet. Major Rasullah, having warned his men not to kill him, began to worry that his ninja wasn't coming. Looking through the night vision scope, he scanned the hangar and the barracks, the helicopters and the fighting holes.

Besides the rising-falling of the windsock and the back-forth of the soldiers pacing out their watch, there was no movement. Just as he was about to call off his stakeout, Rasullah heard the beginnings of an artillery strike on the outpost.

Straining to see the extent of the attack through

the scope, he realized that it wasn't artillery at all, but fireworks. Then he heard the voices of his men; they had captured someone. As they came closer, he could see that they were surrounding a single figure dressed in black, their rifles pointed at his head.

When the captive was finally brought in front of him, Major Rasullah could see in his face, in his eyes, that this was the Man, the legendary swordsman that he'd been building in his mind. His lieutenant, Kareem, had the Ninja's weapons: a sword, two knives, a Long Bow and quiver of arrows, and a few other items, including: night vision goggles, and a Bic-lighter.

"That's it?" said Rasullah, "that's all you brought!? Are you crazy?! Or just stupid?!"

The Major was trying to belittle the silent warrior in front of his men, and but secretly he was in awe, thinking: this man will attack an unknown fortress with only a sword and bow?! I may not able to beat this man.

But he quickly chased the thoughts from his mind: of course I will beat him!

I am superior! This man is obviously insane.

With Rasullah's prisoner loaded in the Hip, Stepkavic started the engines; it was just a short hop back to the base. From the air everything looked okay at the outpost, and Stepkavic slowed down to begin the descent.

Don't stop," the Major said, "continue flying west, to the Bamiyan Valley."

Stepkavic hesitated, giving him a look of confusion, but Rasullah had already concluded that abandoning his post, and taking the Mi-8, would mean the end of his military career.

"That is an order Corporal," he said.

Jack Randall lifted off in the Mi-24 to follow the flying bus, when three of the Afghan-communists climbed in to the remaining Hind to pursue him.

The Krokodil was only two meters off the ground when a grenade, hidden in its engine compartment, detonated; it was instantly engulfed in flames, and careened through the open hangar door where it crashed into the far wall, killing those aboard, and four others in the hangar.

The seventeen surviving DRA soldiers quickly realized the gravity of their situation: surely one of the mujahideen groups in the nearby mountains had seen the explosions, and would be coming out to investigate, to see what they could scavenge.

The Afghan soldiers packed the only KamAZ truck left by the Soviets, with RPGs and NSV DShK 12.7 mm heavy machine-guns and Kalashnikovs and ammunition and food and whatever else they could find, and tore several bed sheets into strips, to fashion white flags.

The Hip landed an hour and a half later, and Rasullah led his prisoner off the transport helicopter.

When Toshi saw the two giant Buddhas carved

in the cliff, his mouth fell open.

"What is this place?"

"These are the Bamiyan Buddhas!" replied Rasul-lah.

Toshi had seen the Maitreyan Buddha statue of the Bingling Temple Caves, in Gansu, China, but these were bigger and much older.

They were still in very good condition. They were carved directly into the sandstone cliffs; the face and hands were coated with a mixture of straw and plaster.

Toshi forgot where he was, and what he was doing.

"Meditation will only lead to acceptance, not understanding..." his father's words from long ago echoed in his head.

And suddenly he was at the dying man's bed-side to hear his final words.

"Hitoshi," only Toshi's father ever called him by his full name, "I'm sorry that I pushed you so hard when you were young...I'm sorry that I did not encourage you to spend more time with your mother, especially when she was dying...I don't know why, but I never thought she would die, not before me anyway. I never told you, but she saved my life, right after you were born. And doing so is probably where her sickness came from...I hope by now you know that she loved you more than her life itself.

"I have one more thing to tell you," his father whispered, "I have always told you that you would only find the meaning of your life on the battle-field," the old man strained to breathe, "but I was wrong..."

Rasullah did not expect this reaction. He had not brought Toshi to the Bamiyan Valley to have a religious experience.

"I was born in this Valley, a Hazara Twelver," he said, "I was orphaned at age nine when my village was attacked by a group of marauding Pashtun tribesmen. Two years later, I was taken to Kabul by a wealthy Afghan-Communist landowner.

At first I marveled at my good fortune, being rescued from utter poverty and certain starvation was a miracle. But once back on the rich man's estate, I was a slave to him. Nothing more than a servant-houseboy, under the tutelage of a cruel butler. As the years progressed, I grew bigger and stronger.

"When I was seventeen years old, I assumed the role of groundskeeper. Two years later, the landowner died and his widow freed me to join the Democratic Republic of Afghanistan's army.

"In addition to learning the military arts, I also received a general education; my favorite subject was History.

"After I discovered that the Hazara people of central Afghanistan are the direct descendents of Genghis Khan and his army, I learned the martial arts of the Mongols. That was fourteen years before the failing Pro-Marxist government called on the USSR to assist them in putting down the rural insurgency.

"Now I am called the Afghan Executioner, my methods for extracting information from the Pashtuns and the Tajiks are well-known and feared by them. I will never kill enough of them to consider myself even though. Never.

"But today, my destiny has been revealed to me, my whole life I have trained and waited patiently to face you, the ancient enemy of my people. So prepare to die! The 'divine winds' will not save you this time."

Rasullah drew his sword, and held it with both hands over his head. His arms were like the two sides of an isosceles triangle.

Toshi looked as if he had just awakened from a dream. He saw his sword, lying on the ground in front of him, and he saw the man in the Afghan-Communist uniform poised to strike.

"I do not want to fight here," said Toshi.

"You do not have a choice," Rasullah sneered.

Though he didn't want to fight, Toshi was not a fool; he picked up the sword and stuck it through his belt, and looked into Rasullah's eyes.

"I will say this only once, if you attack me, I will kill you without a fight."

Toshi meant this as a warning, but Rasullah took it as a challenge and he stepped forward to within striking distance.

As Rasullah began to follow through with his chop, Toshi remembered his father's toyama-ryu, and drew his sword with lightning speed.

It flashed from his belt and whipped through the air, passing underneath the chin of the Hazara-Mongol. Once his arm had fully extended, it snapped back like a bow string, and he re-sheathed the sword.

Rasullah's face was crossed with a look of utter surprise. The thin slice across his throat became a gaping slash as his head rolled back, falling to the ground, and his body fell forward.

The other DRA soldiers panicked when their leader fell, and began firing their Kalashnikovs at Toshi; he dove behind a large rock out-cropping.

After the longest five minutes of his life, with a constant barrage of bullets keeping him pinned down, a lone Hind flew up over the ridge, right over the Japanese swordsman's ducking head.

Before the soldiers could register the situation, Jack mowed them down with the gunship's chain gun.

As Toshi stood up, a discharge of hot brass shell casings rained down on him.

21

I landed the Hind next to the Mi-8, shut it down, and climbed out with my shotgun ready; Toshi came walking out from behind some rocks.

"Hey all right, I found you!" I said.

He didn't answer, but had a look of worry on his face, he was staring over my shoulder. Then he was pointing excitedly, and his lips were moving like he was yelling something; a warning?

I couldn't hear him though, the only thing I could hear was that familiar song:

Sometimes the lights are shining on me...
Other times I can barely see...
Lately it occurs to me...
What a long, strange trip it's been...

Since '71 in the Quang Nam Province-Vietnam,

that song has been my early warning bell, I've learned to listen for it, and it's saved my ass more than once, so I knew something was up; then, right behind me, I heard an assault rifle's action cycle.

I spun around and pumped two shells of double-ought buck into a Soviet as he was coming out of the Hip. He went down...

"Hey Jack!" Toshi waved, and ran over, "You got him! You came at just the right time!"

The soldiers I'd just fragged with the chain-gun weren't wearing Soviet uniforms, and now that I saw them better, didn't even look like Russians.

"These soldiers are Afghan-Communists, Democratic Republic of Afghanistan," he said, "their leader is over there," he pointed back, "minus his head...he spoke to me in Japanese, to these soldiers in Dari, Afghan-Farsi, and he spoke to the pilot you blasted by the transport helicopter in Russian."

Toshi's head went down and his voice got real quiet. "I told him I didn't want to fight here."

He didn't say anything else; he turned and walked over to the edge of the cliff.

We were parked on a ridge looking across what looked like an old road, and more than three hundred meters away, on the other side, were the two giant sandstone Buddhas Pik had told me about.

Toshi just sat there, in the lotus position, facing them. I didn't bother him, and he didn't say anything for a few hours.

"Figure the Soviets probably left their base this

morning with a full tank," I said, more for my own ears than Toshi's.

"About a hundred kilometers from Mehtar Lam to Sra Kala, another hundred back, and then two-hundred-ten or so kilometers here. And I'm pretty sure, that the range on this Bird, fully-fueled, is about four-hundred-fifty kilometers, so if my math is correct, we've only got about forty kilometers worth of fuel left."

I scavenged the Hip, inside and out, detaching one of the full external fuel tanks, as well as the meter-long section of rubber hosing that connected it to the fuel pump. I also found Pik's sixty-five kilos of Afghan brown.

After I'd finished refueling, I turned the back-up generator on long enough to read the fuel gauge, and see that we had almost three quarters of a tank.

"We've got plenty of gas now," I said.

I wanted to wait until dark for the return flight. I built a fire, and raided the Hip's survival kit for some canned food and bottled water.

Once it started getting dark, Toshi came back over to the fire. I passed him a couple open cans, and bottles of water.

He started on them right away, and then went inside the Hip to collect his weapons and other equipment. He also took the rifles that were inside, and put them in the back of the Hind to bring back to the mujahideen.

"So no one on the ground sees us, I'll be sure to

get some altitude. I'm worried that when we pass that airbase on the left," I pointed, "I think it's Bagram Air Base, they might call us to see what's up? Do you speak Russian?"

"A few words, but I am not fluent, I could not fool a native speaker."

He held up the radio Jafir gave me when he dropped us off.

"This is one of the walkie-talkies I gave them; it's one of a pair. Jafir has the other one, they are secure satellite communicators. The Soviets won't be able to listen in to any of our communications."

I got an idea about how to use his information to get by the airbase.

"Thanks for coming to get me, Jack."

"Of course I wasn't going to leave you," I said, "you wouldn't have left me."

"I think I have had enough killing."

That's pretty much all he said until we got back in the Hind.

When we lifted off, I climbed to about four kilometers, hoping that we'd be high enough to avoid antiaircraft fire from any mujahideen groups that we flew over, of course, at that altitude; the flying tank we were in would be pretty tough. Unless they had surface-to-air-missiles, we'd be alright.

It was definitely possible they had missiles, but I was hopeful that they didn't.

"Flying east," I said, "in a straight line, we've got about one hundred-fifty kilometers until we pass Bagram Air Base, probably about forty-five minutes. So, I want you to get Jafir on the hand-held radio, and without going into too much detail, tell him we're going to need someone who can talk to Bagram Tower for us, if and when they call."

Toshi got Jafir on the radio in no time, and passed it to me.

"There is a defected DRA officer in Sra Kala," said Jafir, "arrived this evening, he is fluent in Russian, but does not speak English. I will get him."

"Hold on, are you sure we can trust him?" I said.

"I hope so, he is my cousin; I have known him my whole life. Yes, you can trust him."

"But Jafir, I thought, cousin and enemy, was the same word in Pashto."

"No-no, not enemy, rival, cousin and rival share the same word, but do not worry; I told you we are not Pashtun."

He left and when he came back, I put Toshi on.

"The pilot was Corporal Stepkavic," he told Jafir, "he was flying escort for an Mi-8, Major Rasullah of the DRA was in command, we left from Mehtar Lam Outpost. I'm going to put this radio right up next to the ship's mic."

And about three minutes later:

"ВНИМАНИЕ! ВНИМАНИЕ! НЛО, ЕТО БАЗА БАГРАМ, НЕМЕДЛЕННО НАЗОВИТЕ СЕБЯ МАТЬ ВАШУ !!!"

"БАШНЯ, Я КРОКОДИЛ ПЯТЬ СЕМЬ ШЕСТЬ, ГОВОРИТ КАПИТАН СТЕПКОВИЧ, БЫЛИ В СОПРОВОЖДЕНИИ ПРИКРЫТИЯ МИ-ВОСЕМЬ С ГЕНЕРАЛОМ РАСУЛОМ И ДВЕНАДЦАТЬ ТИ СПЕЦНАЗОВЦЕВ, Б....! ЛЕТЕЛИ С ДАЛЬНЕГО ПОСТА МАХТАР ЛАМ НА БАЗУ КОДАЛАК, Б....! ИДЕМ ДОМОЙ, БЛИН! ВСЕ ОТБОЙ."

"ПЯТЬ СЕМЬ ШЕСТЬ, НОЧНЫЕ ПОЛЕТЫ ОТМЕНЕНЫ. МАТЬ ВАШУ !!!"

"ИЗВИНИ БРАТ, Я ЗНАЮ. СЛУЖБА БЕЗОПАСТНОСТИ ОБРАТИЛАСЬ К НАМ, Б....! ОНИ ДУМАЮТ, ЧТО ДУХИ ГОТОВЯТ АТАКУ. МАТЬ ИХ!"

"ДОБРО, ДЕРЖИТЕ НАС В КУРСЕ, ПРОДОЛЖАЙТЕ ПОЛЕТ, ОТБОЙ. МАТЬ ВАШУ !!!"

"ПЯТЬ СЕМЬ ШЕСТЬ ПОНЯЛ, УХОДИМ. Б....! ОТБОЙ."

Then the radio went quiet.

"Was that it?" I whispered.

Toshi shrugged.

"That is it for now," said Jafir, "they may come back, we will stand by for a few minutes in case."

Ten minutes went by.

"You are probably all clear for a while," he said, "call back if you need to."

He clicked off.

"That was easy enough," I said. "What did they say?"

"I think it was something like:

'attention unknown aircraft, this is Bagram. Identify yourself…'

'This is Krokodil-576 flying escort for Spetsnas Troopers from Mehtar Lam Outpost to Kodolak Field Base…'

'You should not be flying at night…'

'Sorry sir, intelligence suggests an attack on Mehtar Lam is imminent…'

"I am not sure about the rest, some curse words or slang."

We were flying two-hundred-forty kilometers per hour, but after passing the air base, I pushed it up to three-hundred-twenty. I was going back to

Mehtar Lam outpost to get some ground reference.

A half-hour later, I spotted the still-smoldering remains of the outpost hangar from earlier that morning—I couldn't believe it was still the same day.

Toshi called Jafir again.

"Hover directly over the bombed out hangar," said Jafir, "and facing exactly southeast, you will see in the distance, a blue and red blinking light."

Toshi eagle eyed it, and pointed.

"Yeah, I got it. "

"Right below that light is the ridge where I dropped you off this afternoon; keep that light on your right side. Jalalabad Air Base is on the other side, you may see their lights further west, and my cousin is still here if they call you. In twenty minutes we will set fire to the poppy fields, they are empty now. Khatol harvested the remaining opium this morning, and the chemists are processing it now. They expect twenty-five kilos. Did you get the other back?"

"Yes I did!" I said triumphantly, "we'll be watching for the fire, see you shortly."

We didn't hear from Jalalabad Air Base, and thirty-five minutes later, Toshi spotted the burning fields and we landed safely. I cut the engines as soon as we touched down.

Mahmoud, Khaleed, Jafir and his cousin Maruk, and a few others from the group were there to meet us. They had a trailer behind one of the pickups, big enough to carry the Hind.

And while the main rotor was still spinning, Khaleed and Jafir stopped it with an eight-foot pine 4x4 and then started to remove it.

I'm sure the five bladed prop was probably about three thousand kilos or more, not to mention almost twenty meters in diameter. They loaded it on the trailer with a makeshift crane that resembled a reinforced telephone pole, and covered it in less than an hour.

On until dawn, Toshi and I told the others about our last twenty-four hours: starting at the Mehtar Lam Outpost, ending at the Bamiyan Valley, where Toshi killed Major Rasullah.

They all knew him.

22

I had just gotten to sleep, when the rooster started crowing.

The night before Toshi had asked me to let him tell Mahmoud of his decision to leave, so he walked with him to the Mosque that morning. I was awake, but still in my sleeping bag when he left.

An hour later, Mahmoud came back and told me that he wanted to leave for Peshawar the next evening.

After doing my push-ups and sit-ups, and eating some nan and honey, I went to check on that last twenty-five kilos. It was still drying out, but the chemists said it would be ready by later on that afternoon. Khatol made it clear to me that she'd bring it over as soon as she wrapped it.

For the rest of the day, I daydreamed about getting back to Big Wave Bay. It felt like it'd been a year since I'd gotten any surfing in.

Toshi came back from hiking around in the Wach Bandar Mountains right before sunset.

He said he talked to Mahmoud that morning about leaving.

"He wasn't mad, and seemed to understand. I also told him that I had $25,000 hidden in the handle of my sword that I wanted to give to the villagers so they could buy more livestock."

"What did Mahmoud say to that?"

"He said that he understood me wanting to leave, and that although he could not refuse the of-fer for the livestock, it was not necessary for me to pay to leave. When I insisted that I wanted to, he took me over to the goatherds and told them what I meant to do. They knew of an animal auction that was being held today in a neighboring village, where they could buy goats, chickens, oxen, and camels. A number of young men came over, put a wagon caravan together and they left."

"Camels? I stopped him, "what do they do with camels?"

"I think they milk them."

I knew they didn't eat Camels, but I didn't know they milked them. The group returned a few hours later with twenty-five goats, seven oxen, ten wire coops–each holding four chickens and five camels, with plenty of money left over to get more when they were available.

Khatol and a few of the other older women of the village prepared a small meal to show Toshi and me their gratitude.

"It's called Kofta Nahkod," said Jafir. "It is made of ground beef, rolled into meatballs, in a soup of Chick Peas-Nakhwed shorwa, seasoned with salt and pepper, crushed mint, and onion."

I noticed they only made enough "naked coda" for the two of us, everyone else had chicken.

23

Later that night Toshi, Mahmoud, and I, along with a few of the others were sitting around the fire.

"The Soviets call us barbarians," Jafir started the discussion, "because sometimes they find one of their soldiers with his lips or nose missing, or otherwise mutilated, yet when they fire missiles or drop bombs and kill an entire village of nursing mothers and children and old people, they call it Modern Warfare or Collateral Damage."

I noticed that the mujahideen didn't take prisoners, at least not that I saw. That mutilation Jafir mentioned was a psychological tool used to scare young Russians into not fighting; similar to how the Viet Cong used to mutilate GIs. A scare tactic used since the beginning of warfare itself, I'm sure.

Toshi told me about Khatol cutting up the Russian who shit on her plates, and I'd gotten a few comments from the farmers about scalping that Soviet. They all told me he deserved it; he did, I don't really regret it, but I do admit my emotions, at the time, were out of control, not very professional at all.

I mentioned that I had been worried, the night before while flying the Hind from Bamiyan, that some of the other mujahideen groups might have SAMs.

"Your American CIA has actually just begun shipping the shoulder-fired Stinger surface to air missiles to a group in the Northwest Frontier Province in Pakistan," said Khalid.

"America is only helping us because it hurts the Russians," Mahmoud added. "Have you heard the saying, 'the enemy of my enemy is my friend'? The Soviet Union has been the only competition for the United States since the end of World War II, it has been said that the nuclear attacks on Hiroshima and Nagasaki, were more to warn the Soviets than to defeat the already defeated Japanese.

"The Russians gave aid to the enemies of America in Vietnam – and now America is having its revenge. But I do worry, when the Russians have been beaten and are gone, will America abandon us?"

"What do you think about the Arabs who came to fight," I asked Mahmoud.

"Most are answering the call to Jihad as demanded by Allah, but some are fighting simply to appear more Muslim; some are fighting each other more than they are fighting the Russians.

"And it is forbidden by Allah for a Muslim to kill another Muslim. Sometimes the Sunni kill the Shia, saying they are not really Muslims anyway, and sometimes the Shia kill the Sunni claiming the same thing. They are both wrong, and will be judged by Allah. This war we are fighting with the Soviets is a chance for Sunni and Shia to unite, we must unite."

"Unite?! Are you joking?!" said the villager named Abdul, "the Arabs that come to fight, kill more Arabs than Russians! Just like in the Arab-Jew war! Arabs killed more Arabs than Jews that is why they lost."

"We are Pashtun, then we are Sunni," a villager named Jandol added, "we are as strict as we need to be. We follow the haditha of Hanafi, the oldest of the four schools, but the Wahhabi pick through them all until they find an answer that best suits their particular situation, we pray five times a day, and we observe Ramadan."

Ramadan was some kind of period of atonement; a month-long ritual of fasting during daylight hours. It had something to do with the first crescent moon of a new lunar year. It's time of observance changes every year, but this year it was from about the middle of February until the middle of March.

The villagers who I saw on a daily basis seemed pretty strict or devoted to the fasting, but I didn't see Mahmoud's group for weeks at a time so I don't know how they did. It was very cold though to be starving yourself.

Jandol continued, "Throughout history we have always placed great importance on our artistic tendencies, but they do not approve of art, they do not approve of music and dance. They call us apostates, but our culture is six-thousand years old, and we have practiced the same Islam for almost thirteen-hundred years with little or no change. Some of the other older chieftains appreciate their strict orthodoxy, their almost cruel intolerance."

One of the men that didn't speak English started talking then, and Mahmoud translated so I could understand.

"These Arabs are brave, but to them the goal of fighting the jihad is not being victorious but being martyred. And they go about blowing everything up, we do not have that many decent roads and bridges to begin with, but they do not seem to understand or do not care that we Pashtun need the roads and bridges to transport our crops to market. We have not only to fight the jihad, but also feed our families, earn our livings."

I have heard of the fight between the Shia and the Sunni. When I was getting ready to come to Afghanistan, Pik tutored me a little about Islam, and gave me a few books to thumb through. But I still wasn't sure what their fight was all about.

When Jafir, Khalid, and I were driving back from Kabul a few months ago, he mentioned that he and Khalid were not Pashtuns, but Tajiks.

"We are Shia not Sunni," he said. "We have joined Mahmoud's mujahideen group, Khalid and I, because we are friends, and because he is my sister's husband."

I composed what little I knew into a question-statement for Mahmoud.

"The Sunni follow the life and teachings of the Prophet Mohammed and the Shia follow the laws of Islam as given by the Koran."

"That is a very good explanation," he said, "better than I would have expected from a Westerner, but it is not quite complete. No, it goes back to the beginning of Islam."

He gave me a long story about unnamed successors and misinformed historical vengeance. It sounded a lot like the old Hatfield-McCoy feud, where no one on either side could really remember what they were fighting about.

Fighting over religion doesn't make much sense to me anyway; it's bullshit. Religion is a tool used by governments and rulers, they get everybody to believe the same thing and it's much easier to tell them what to do.

On the Indian Reservation in South Dakota, where I grew up, the Lakota religion is just like the religion of every other Indian Tribe in America: not really a religion at all, but a way of life. God is called 'The Great Mystery.'

"We are just people," my grandfather used to say, "the youngest animal, we cannot know the mind of our creator."

He told me a story about a great old chief who was once asked by a young missionary why he didn't want to learn the white man's knowledge.

"It seems you only teach each other to fight over God," the chief replied, "we don't want to learn that."

I'm not really a Catholic anymore; I went to a parochial boarding school for a couple years, sixth grade through tenth grade, and I did pretty well. But a few days before my fifteenth birthday, I went to the chapel to pray.

Thinking that I was alone, I began speaking out loud. I'd started to doubt if there was a God listening to my prayers.

"You're not real are you?! Here I pray to you every day, and I follow all of your commandments, and I just ask that you give me some sign, to tell me that you are there and that you hear me."

But I got no answer.

"There is no God!" I yelled in frustration, and added, "God, go to Hell!"

From the back of the small chapel, a short elderly priest came running out to confront me.

"No! You will not blaspheme in here! Get out of here!" he screamed at me.

They called my father to come pick me up, and I was expelled from the school. That day was the end of me believing in any organized religion.

I finally worked up the courage to ask Mahmoud.

"When does Allah sanction a Holy War?"

He looked at me, as if surprised.

"War can never be Holy," he said, "jihad has been misinterpreted for many years, and unfortunately this mistake has not been corrected.

"In the Koran, there are two jihads, the lesser jihad and the greater jihad. Both refer to struggles. The lesser jihad is a struggle, a personal struggle, to become a better Muslim, the greater jihad is an armed struggle to overcome an oppressor who is trying to take your land and/or destroy your religion."

"But aren't the mujahideen soldiers of God?" I said.

Again he looked at me.

"God does not need soldiers. The Holy Koran's twenty-ninth surah, The Spider, says: 'those who fight for Allah, only fight for themselves. Allah is independent of man.' No, mujahideen does not mean soldiers of God, it means strugglers, or those who Jihad.

"I have heard people say the Communists are atheists, they do not believe in God. But I don't think that all Communists are atheists, true atheists. I have killed many Soviet soldiers, and seen many others be killed by my Afghan brothers, and most of them have prayed to their God while they are dying. Begging for mercy or forgiveness for their earthly transgressions, just like any other believer.

"So I do not believe that the Russians are trying to attack Islam. Although we have lived as allies for many years, they have invaded Afghanistan and are occupying our lands and killing our people because the Soviets want to expand the Russian Empire, and gain access to the warm water ports of Pakistan, with no regard for the Afghans."

For the last few months I've been wondering: who is this Allah? It turns out that Allah is the God of Abraham, the same God that the Jews and the Christians pray to.

There was a tall, skinny Arab who came to fight the Soviets. One morning back in December, I was standing outside, right about here, soaking up the warmth of the fire. He walked past me, and I greeted him with the only Arabic I know.

"Salaam alaykum."

He stopped, looked at me, and then started screaming at me furiously. I didn't know what he was saying, but I could tell he was angry about something. I asked Mahmoud about him.

"They call him the Sheik. When he first came to Afghanistan, he stayed in the southern Paktia province, in Jaji. Now I am not sure where he is… probably somewhere between Jalalabad and Tora Bora.

"We've killed many Russians together. And yes, he hates non-Muslims, especially Westerners.

"He is from Saudi Arabia, from a family that is very close to the Royal Family. They are very rich, very powerful. I have much respect for him because he could be anywhere in the world, being serviced by rooms full of beautiful women, but instead he is here fighting these infidels with us. He is a hero to many Afghans and to many Muslims throughout the world."

That was all he said about the Sheik.

24

The others went to sleep, but Toshi, Mahmoud and I, stayed up for a while yet.

It was quiet, except for the crackling of the fire. I broke the silence.

"Let's play a game, the three of us tell a story, a story about something real that happened, or maybe retell someone else's story the way you remember hearing it. We'll each get a few minutes to think of a story, tell it in the first person. I'll go first."

Toshi and Mahmoud agreed, and then we were quiet again, getting our stories straight. Right away I knew the story I wanted to tell. I'd wanted to tell this story for a long time, since I first heard it, but I never had.

"This is my Grandfather's story."

I reached into my pocket, pulled out my medicine pouch, and fished around inside it for a minute, finding the tarnished brass Seventh Calvary insignia, and passed it to Mahmoud.

"He told me this story when I was sixteen years old, and he died the next day, he was one-hundred years old. His story takes place June, 1876, in the Southeast corner of Montana.

"I remembered my Grandfather, wearing his black Stetson, the wisdom in his eyes, and the warmth in his voice when he called me by the name he had given me when I was one-year-old: Looks-With-Wonder."

I had lived for twelve winters. It was the time of the Sundance. We were camped in the valley of the Greasy Grass. There were two camps; one camp was for the warriors, and the other camp was for the women, the children, and the elders.

The warrior camp was just on the other side of a ridge, then came our camp, and then came a small forest.

One morning, me and my friend, Half Elk, were in the forest collecting firewood for my mother's fire. The night before there had been a giveaway and we had each received a new stone axe. We were chopping up small trees and branches when we heard some riders approaching.

The fact that we heard them at all told us they were strangers. We could hear them talking to each other, but didn't know what they were saying. We climbed into trees to hide.

When the riders came into view, there were three of them–soldiers. Two of them wore the uniforms of cavalry soldiers, and the other wore a fine buckskin coat and a wide brimmed black hat with gold ornaments on it, I saw him and thought of the man the warriors called Longhair, some called him Goldhair

Longhair was known for attacking women and children and old people, so he was much feared among them. But I just thought he was a coward, I didn't think he was crazy. There were almost four-thousand warriors, Lakota, Dakota, Nakota, and Cheyenne, just over the ridge. He must not have known.

The three of them seemed to be arguing about something. Then finally, Longhair took off his fine coat and black hat, and gave them to one of the other men, and that man took off his cap and jacket and passed them back. Before he put them on though, the third man came over and cut all of his gold hair off.

When he put on the Army cap and jacket, he was no longer recognizable as Longhair. The other soldier, who had traded his uniform for a Long-hair's also had long hair, but it wasn't as golden.

When he put on the buckskin coat and black hat of Longhair, he looked just like him, before he cut his hair off.

After the exchange, the three got back on their horses and rode off in different directions. The new Longhair and the other soldier went one way, and the old Longhair went the other.

We climbed down the trees. Half Elk said we should go after them to find out what they were doing. He wanted that buckskin coat, so he followed the fake Longhair and the cutter.

I followed the real Longhair, on foot. I followed him, quiet and out of sight as he rode through the forest.

He stopped and got off his horse, but did not turn around, I am not sure what he was doing.

With my new stone axe in my right hand, I ran up behind him, still quiet, and as I swung my axe, a gunshot rang out, and he turned around. My axe hit him right in the forehead, killing him instantly.

He crumpled to the ground. I stood there, and stared at him, thinking about all of the people that he had killed and what a monster he was supposed to be. I killed him so easily, broke his head right open and let his brains spill out.

Then I remembered Half Elk and the gunshot I heard. I ran towards the gunshot. I heard many war cries and much hooting, and then much more shooting. The warriors must have heard the gunshot too, and now Hell was breaking loose.

I finally reached Half Elk but he was dead, shot through the eye. I should have known he was going to try to attack both men. He was my friend and I was more worried about killing Longhair so I could be a hero to my tribe, but no one believed me.

The rest of the story I think you know. It was

not a Last Stand, it was a Quick Battle. And they lost.

But now I have seen a hundred winters and I will probably not see another. Never have I been the hero of my tribe, but when I was a boy I killed Custer.

"I knew you were from a family of warriors," said Mahmoud.

I think he liked my game, so much he wanted to go next. Toshi didn't object.

"Are either of you familiar with the painting Remnants of an Army by Lady Elizabeth Butler?"

Then he passed us a postcard with a painting of a lone horseman, beaten and bleeding, riding through a rocky desert mountain pass. I thought it looked like a Charlie Russell painting I'd seen in Grand Forks, Montana when I was a teenager.

"I remember it from a history of contemporary art class I took in University," said Toshi.

"Do you know the story that goes with the painting?"

"January 1842," said Toshi, "the sole survivor of a contingent of British soldiers with their wives and children along with their camps workmen and other noncombatants, around sixteen thousand people if I remember correctly, that were slaughtered by Akbhar Kahn after they surrendered and

were given the promise of a safe passage to Jalalabad. He was an army surgeon I think."

Mahmoud smiled.

"Well, that is the Western side of the story. But
what actually happened is quite different, Muslims
are forbidden to kill innocent noncombatants."

I immediately thought of the Israeli Olympic
athletes who were killed in Munich by Palestinian
Muslims, but I didn't say anything.

"No, the innocents were given safe passage
with an escort of one thousand soldiers, a week before the remaining soldiers, around three thousand
men, were to begin the one-hundred-fifty kilometer march to the Jalalabad Garrison.

"The innocents arrived safely as promised, there
were even several instances that their wagons broke
down and the Kahn's men gave them assistance.

"When the soldiers were to begin their march,
perhaps they thought that they would be hailed as
heroes when they defeated the Kahn's forces. I am
sure they reasoned: surely the British army is much
better equipped than a rural militia.

"My great-grandfather's story goes like this:"

An army of about three thousand British soldiers
attacked us, we were easily ten thousand strong
but they were well-equipped, with repeating rifles,
and cartridge fed cannons.

By the grace of Allah, we stomped them, in
three days. And after we had finished, I went to see

my wife, she was already eight moons pregnant but I had just faced death, and I needed some release.

So I had her, from behind, bent over the wagon. It was very good, and I think it was good for her too. But I must have jostled her too hard, because water gushed out of her.

'The baby is coming!' she said.

I suppose I panicked, I didn't know what to do, all of the midwives were tending to our wounded. I noticed one of the dead men moving around, I immediately went over to kill him.

I was just about to shoot him in the head, when I noticed two small golden ornaments on his collar, it was a snake wrapped around a staff. I had seen that symbol before, but I couldn't remember where.

He opened his eyes and began speaking to me, but I didn't understand his language.

Then he said, 'Ze daktar yam,' I was surprised when he spoke Pashto.

'My wife is giving birth,' I told him.

Then I helped him up and over to my wife. She was laying on the ground by the wagon, with her head propped up on a rock.

'Move that wagon over here closer so she can put her feet on it,' he said.

I did, and she had both legs spread open on the wagon. Then the doctor asked for some blankets and hot water. I gathered what I could and gave them to him. He told her to push, and she began to breathe heavily.

'It is coming,' he said.

And then he said some English words, I could not understand.

He looked agitated, but I did not know what was wrong until I looked. I had three other wives who had each given me sons before and I had always been there to witness the births, so when I saw the feet coming first I knew that was wrong. He took hold of both feet and gently pulled.

When the baby came out, everything looked all right, except the chord was wrapped around its neck, and it wasn't making any noise.

He unwrapped the chord from the infant's neck, and began pumping his chest with his fingers while breathing into its mouth. After a moment, the baby started sputtering, and then started crying. I was so happy; I knew he had just saved my son's life.

Once my wife and newborn were settled, I remembered the doctor. I couldn't kill him now, but I had to get him out of there before the others returned, because they would kill him.

I told him to lie down in the back of the wagon, and I put a blanket over him, the same blanket my wife had just giving birth on—so it was covered with blood.

'Pretend you are dead or you will be dead,' I told him.

I knew my wife would be alright with our son, so I left them and tied another horse to my wagon, and starting riding to Jalalabad. I rode one-hundred kilometers without saying anything. When I realized that no one was following us, I stopped and let him out.

He was covered with my wife's blood, my son's afterbirth. When I was convinced that he would be all right the rest of the way I stopped following him. He rode the rest of the way on horseback.

"That doctor," Mahmoud said, "William Brydon, birthed my father's father."

Finally it was Toshi's turn.

"My story is not as old as either of yours, it is actually my father's story, he told it to me, and now I will tell it to you in his words.

It was August 1945, you were born in June, and your mother, Keiko, had taken you to her parents for a visit, in Tokushima. I was a bachelor again for a week or so.

One year before you were born, I was in the Emperor's army, but I had been injured in the battle for the Philippines at Ormoc Valley, so I was discharged from field service. I had been given service watching/guarding the military prison in my home city, Hiroshima.

It was empty except for nine U.S. Air Force POWs. They had been picked up in the ocean and transferred from another prison, by rail–the harbor was mined by the US–so there was no boat traffic. They were pretty nice guys actually; they said they were farmers from the Midwest of the United States. We played chess–usually it was four or five of them against me; none of them was very good, and I usually beat all of them at once.

It usually got pretty hot in Hiroshima in August and the prison cell was in the basement of the military administration building. The fans did not work that well and there weren't many windows, so sometimes at night I would let them sleep in the atrium outside.

The atrium/yard was a small, 4x6 meter section in the middle of two buildings used especially for prisoners to get exercise and be outside. It was cooler out there than inside the cell and there was only one door with seventy meter shear walls, there was no chance for escape. I would let them out to sleep at around eleven o'clock and go home, returning the next morning at six o'clock to let them back in for breakfast.

But on the night of August 5, after I let them out, I met with several friends of mine who were on leave. And since my family was out of town, I went out with them, drinking and to a cat house. Since I was already married with a child, I just waited for them in the bar, drinking rice wine, and eating spicy bean curd.

They were gone quite a while, so I drank and ate quite a bit. They finally came back at around three o'clock in the morning, and I had to leave to go home for a few hours sleep before getting back to the prison. I made it to work about forty-five minutes late.

When I did make it in to work, I had an upset stomach. I could not let them in because I had to stay in the basement and have very bad geri–diarrhea.

There was a vent going from the atrium to the bathroom I was in, so I could hear them snoring, despite my flatulence. When I was almost finished, I heard an airplane coming. It didn't sound like a Japanese airplane though, and I immediately thought of the firebombing of Tokyo, just the week before.

Just then I could hear some of the POWs waking up outside. They were talking; they could hear the plane too.

'Sounds like a B-29 bomber!' one of them said.

The next sound I heard was almost deafening, an explosion like nothing I'd ever heard before. Then the building started shaking and crumbling. I felt an incredible heat, and the rest of the building came down on top of me, I was trapped inside. After about five days, I was found by your mother who had led the rescue team.

I had no food for that time, but there was a well in the basement of the building so I had plenty of water, and I could breathe. I'm sure the nine Americans were incinerated immediately.

When your mother heard of the bombing, she left you with her parents and rushed back to Hiroshima to find me. She had been there for three days and had been breathing that poisonous air.

"Twenty years later, my mother developed cancer, and she died about six months later. Eighteen years after that, my father also died of cancer, just last year. I have no doubt that their deaths, their cancers, were directly related to that bomb."

Well I did say it was a game, so it's fair to say it was a competition, but I'm not sure who won.

25

My eyes popped open when the rooster started crowing; I was still in my bag next to the burned-out fire. I sat up and looked around to see if anyone else was still out there with me.

"Mahmoud got up a few minutes ago, to pray no doubt," said Toshi, still lying zipped up in his sleeping bag on the other side.

It was almost June, and by the end of the day the temperature would reach the mid to upper thirties, Celsius that is, but overnight the mercury would fall to about ten degrees, so the sleeping bags were warranted. The two of us lounged there, drinking tea and eating nan until about ten o'clock.

Mahmoud came to tell us that we should be ready to leave for Peshawar after nightfall, and that there was a buyer for the Krokodil waiting for us at Dean's Hotel. Mazar was also going to meet us there.

It was dark by the time we were ready to leave Sra Kala. Toshi was saying his goodbyes to some of the villagers. But I knew I'd probably be back next year, so I just told them Toksa, it's one of the only Lakota words I remember, and it means See You Again, or something like that.

On our way out of town, Mahmoud was driving, I was sitting by the window, and despite the cool night, Toshi was riding in back.

"I want to be ready for another ambush." he said.

He'd unzipped his bag all the way, and draped it over him, and even though he said he never wanted to use it again, kept the assault rifle within reach.

Jafir and Khaleed followed behind us towing the Hind. The thirty five kilometers of straight road to Towr Kam went by pretty fast, and as we started up the incline to the Kyhber Pass, I suddenly felt the need to tell Mahmoud the truth about my military service.

"I was a Ranger in Vietnam," I said, "but only for a little more than three-hundred days."

Though he didn't take his attention off the road ahead, he seemed to be looking at me out of the corner of his right eye.

"Don't get me wrong," I added quickly, "I saw a lot of combat in ten months, had forty-two confirmed kills before I got an injury that ended my war."

I waited for a response, but there was none.

"Well the injury was minor," I continued, "but the infection that came with it almost killed me," I looked at him and let my words sink in.

"Anyway, I went to a navy hospital for about five days worth of hard-core antibiotic treatment, and got two-weeks leave for reenlisting. After two weeks in Hong Kong, I was heading to the airbase to catch a transport plane back to the Bush, when I got an opportunity to disappear. It was a total accident, I wasn't looking for it, but I took it, and deserted. That's when I met Pik Hsun."

Again I waited, but still Mahmoud stayed quiet.

"Just wanted to be completely honest with you," I said, and added, "I haven't seen my family, or been back to America since 1970."

"I was born in Sra Kala," he said finally, "the youngest of four; I had two brothers and a sister. My mother got sick and died when I was very young, and my sister, Barik, became my surrogate mother. She was only six years older than me.

My father married her off to his brother's son, Habib, who had grown up with my oldest brother, Hask. She left my father's house to go live with him.

Although she still lived in Sra Kala, I remember being angry for a time, both at my father, for making her leave, and at my cousin, for taking her away from me.

"A few years later, I began to feel the urge to take a wife, but one of my own choosing. I had grown tired of the endless cycles of tribal life: the constant blood-feuds between families and competition among family members, sibling and tribal rivalries. I wanted to leave Sra Kala and go to Kabul.

"The next week, I saw Barik at the Mosque, and asked to speak to her. When I told her of my desire to leave, she told me I should think about it some more first."

"'I understand you,' she said, 'but the others in Sra Kala will judge you a coward for running away, and father will banish you forever.'

"Shortly afterwards, Barik was caught having illicit relations with a man from a neighboring Shinwari village. Pashtunwali is quite severe in cases of adultery; it calls for the immediate deaths of both parties. My father ordered me and my brother, Qadir, to kill Barik, and told my other brother to kill the adulterous man.

"But, I refused to kill my sister. Qadir started screaming at me, accusing me of being a traitor.

"'Father has given you an order! It is for our family's honor! If you do not answer Father's rightful demand for justice, I will kill her myself, but I will kill you first!'

"My father stopped him though. 'No, Qadir leave him, in the morning, you and Hask must go to Kogyani and kill the two apostates, Mahmoud will not be killed, but,' he turned and glared at me, 'you must leave right now and never come back.'

"In no time I was ready to leave, 'Baba, bakhshana ghwarem—I am sorry father,' I said, but he dismissed me with a silent wave, and I started walking to Kabul.

Kogyani is thirty kilometers from Sra Kala, so I stopped there to warn Barik. But she had already fled to Pakistan.

"Years later, I found out that Barik had gone, with the Shinwari-Kogyani man, to the United States. I also found out that my father had become chieftain of Sra Kala and that my brother Hask had been killed in a fight over another man's wife.

"In Kabul I worked for ten years as a carpenter and janitor at the university, that's where I met Jafir and Khaleed. Jafir introduced me to his sister, we married and Mazar was born. Soon after, I began studying veterinarian medicine.

"When the Soviets invaded, the bigger cities of Afghanistan were not bombed. Other than the increased presence of the Communists, life in Kabul was the same. The more rural areas of the country, however, the tribal areas, were pounded ceaselessly for the first year of the occupation. Sra Kala was targeted, and my father and remaining brother were killed in a rocket attack.

"When I rushed back to help with the reconstruction effort, the village's new chieftain, who had been a friend of my father's, remembered me and asked me to lead a mujahideen group to over-see security in Sra Kala—not to provoke another Soviet attack, but to restore order to the once peaceful village.

"It had been almost thirty years since I'd left, since I'd been banished for not killing my sister, but I finally came back to help the people of Sra Kala.

"You've met Mazar, and you know he is my son. I never wanted him to be influenced by Pashtun tribal life, so when I came here two years ago, I asked his mother, my wife, to take him to Peshawar so he could finish his education."

Just as he was finishing, we pulled into outer Peshawar.

26

Peshawar was the same crowded, noisy, dirty place I remembered.

At Dean's, we met with the Krok buyer, he was from somewhere in Indonesia, I didn't talk to him. He wanted the Hind for private security at his estate, he was going to trail the bird to Keti Bandar, a small port town south of Karachi, and put it on a boat.

He must have a big spread to need a helicopter for security, I thought. He only gave Mahmoud $1.5 million for it; I'm sure he knew that he could've gotten twice that, but this way it was just a simple, cash and carry deal.

It was about eight o'clock by then, and Mazar hadn't shown up yet. So Mahmoud, Jafir and Khaleed went to the mosque, saying they would keep an eye on the trucks.

Toshi and I got the same suite at the hotel, and

I took the barrel-duffel full of heroin with us. We went to the restaurant for a late supper.

After we ate, I remembered that Pik had given me a number to call when I was ready to come back. I called from the room, it wasn't Pik's number.

"Go to the Landi Town district of Karachi," an unfamiliar voice said, "and look for Korangi Harbor, check in to the Crescent Wharf Inn and await further instructions."

I knew that Pik was just being cautious.

After that, Toshi and I spent a few hours looking at a map of Pakistan, finding Karachi and Korangi Harbor.

Karachi was a little more than eleven-hundred kilometers south of Peshawar, and Korangi Harbor was forty kilometers southeast of the Port of Karachi.

That night I took about a forty-five minute shower, my first shower since October.

We got up early the next morning, had some breakfast out front, and went to meet the others.

Mazar had shown up the night before, after Toshi and I had gone to the hotel.

I told Mahmoud the instructions I'd gotten from Kowloon, and he suggested that Mazar and Jafir escort Toshi and me to Karachi.

"They both speak Urdu, and can readily pose as guides for a wealthy Japanese businessman and his bodyguard, to dispel any suspicions."

It sounded like a good idea to me.

I told Mahmoud and Khaleed that I'd see 'em in about a year, and Toshi told them both good-bye, and we loaded up. We took the Grand Trunk Road out of Peshawar, they were going to take a detour to Dara Adam Khel to order some more rifles before heading back, so we followed behind them to the cutoff. Mahmoud waved once more as he forked off to the right, and Jafir thumped the horn a few times as we pulled away. It was half past ten in the morning.

An hour later, Jafir pulled over to let me jump in back with Mazar. When we started up again, he was able to drive pretty fast, making it difficult to hear Mazar as he told me about the road.

"The GT Road," he said, "is an eighteen-hundred kilometer highway that snakes through Pakistan's Northwest Frontier Province and leads to Karachi. It began as a simple caravan path over three-hundred years ago, and was paved by the British after World War II."

He was a really smart kid, I hoped he'd be able to get away from this war, do something with his life. I know Mahmoud wanted that too, in fact since I met him I'd always had the feeling that Mahmoud wasn't really interested in all that fighting for glory stuff and after the conversation we had on the drive to Peshawar, I knew I was right.

We stopped again to get some gas and road munchies. It was five o'clock and we were about halfway to Karachi. Jafir wanted to stretch out in back for a while, and Mazar volunteered to drive.

Toshi offered to switch places with me, but I liked riding in back, so I declined.

The night air was getting warmer as we were getting closer to the ocean, so I was pretty comfortable riding in the back of the truck, besides it would give them, Toshi and Mazar, a chance to talk some, both were into math.

I fell asleep; woke up around one o'clock in the morning in the rain, as we were driving through the Karachi suburbs. Jafir was sitting up, and since we were going much slower now, city driving, I asked him if he knew where we were.

"We are not far," he said, "fifteen or twenty minutes."

I remembered driving through Bangkok years before, and Karachi was probably twice as big. I asked if he had been here before.

"Yes, I have family and friends who live here, some from Afghanistan who fled when the Soviets invaded, and some from before that."

Twenty minutes later we pulled up in front of the Crescent Wharf Inn.

It was late, but there was a light on in the hotel office, so I went in and got two rooms, four beds. Once we had unloaded everything, Jafir and Mazar went to a local mosque–those things stay open all the time I guess. Toshi wanted to sleep in a bed for a while. I, on the other hand, was wide awake, and it had been almost a year since I had been able to go out and drink a beer at a bar. There was a Samurai in the next bed to guard the heroin, so I figured I could go find a beer, one beer.

I crossed the street in front of the hotel, and could hear moving water; looking toward the sound though, I couldn't really see, too dark. But there was a lot going on the other way: hookers, drug dealers, sex theaters, and nightclubs serving alcohol everywhere. It was still Pakistan of course, an Islamic state, but I guess because it was a port city it was impossible to enforce the religious laws.

I ducked in to a little bar with a big neon sign with red block letters that read Global Spirits, and ordered a beer in the bottle. I drank my beer and made small talk with the other bar-goers, mostly American Navy sailors, then wandered back to the hotel to sleep for a couple hours.

I woke at nine when Toshi came back in from making a coffee/tea run to a bakery up the block.

"I picked you up a few fig pastries too."

He set my coffee and a brown paper grocery sack on the small round table in the corner of the room. I got out of bed, slowly, got some shorts on, and made my way over to the table. I had never been much of a coffee drinker, but this was real good coffee.

The grocery-sack held three pastries and a napkin. Good pastries, but kinda sticky. When I reached for the napkin, I saw there was a note scribbled on it: Municipal Docks, Korangi Harbor, Noon.

I asked if he'd seen the person who packed the bag, or if they said anything else.

"No, I did not see or talk to anyone. Why?"

I showed him the note, and he was embarrassed for not paying closer attention to his surroundings.

Jafir knew right where we were supposed to go.

"Only five minutes down the wharf."

We checked-out at about half past eleven, and found a spot where we could park the truck right across from the municipal docks. I wasn't sure what to expect, so I decided to go alone, armed of course, but leaving the heroin in the truck with the others.

At noon I still didn't see anyone familiar, the docks were real crowded with people buying and selling stuff, food and crafts, or carrying stuff to the market. I guess the whole area of the docks was a bazaar.

Just when I started thinking that I must be in the wrong place, I was sure I caught a glimpse of a face from my past. Once he saw me, and I saw the flicker of recognition in his eyes, I knew it was Chiang Mai.

It had been eight or nine years since I'd seen him last; in his mid to late 50s, short and stocky, a little heavier and a little grayer than the last time I saw him.

He was my oldest living friend and I was happy to see him.

27

Not only was I surprised that Chiang Mai was here picking me up, but when I followed him back to where his boat was tied up, I saw Johnny and Joey Chan, Pik's nephews, sitting on the back deck of the Triple CJ.

The Chans were identical twins and kung fu champions; I said that Toshi looked like a Japanese Bruce Lee, but the Chans looked just like Bruce Lee.

I'll give you a little background. The Triple CJ is a twenty meter trawler that was owned by Captain Cornelius Cecil Jonas, Neil, who saved my life in Hong Kong, 1971, that's when I deserted. That same day I met Chiang Mai, and a few days later went to work for Pik smuggling on the Triple CJ. Neil got killed in 1976, but that's another story.

What a reunion! I almost forgot about the others.

"Hold on," I said, "I want to introduce you to a few people, I'll bring them down here."

"No," he stopped me, "I better come with you, we can't let anyone come aboard the boat, except for you and Toshi."

It almost went right over my head, but I caught it. How did he know about Toshi? I stood there perplexed, I scrunched-up my brow as I looked at the faces of my three long-lost friends; instantly I could tell that the Chans had no idea why I was looking at them so weird, but, Chiang Mai's look, told me that he knew he'd let a cat out of a bag. He wasn't too worried about it though.

"Before we go up there," he said, "I told Pik that I'd get you to call him when I met you. He'll explain everything."

I got Pik on the ship's radio; I guess it was about five in the afternoon in Kowloon.

"Hey Jack, how's it going? Long time no talk." It was the same old Pik.

"All right man, doin' all right. What are you having me followed?"

That was the only way I could think of that Chiang Mai would know I was traveling with Toshi.

"I'm just watching out for you."

"How long have you been watching me," I asked.

"Well, I wouldn't say I've been watching you

really, I'm in Kowloon, but Mahmoud called me, before you left Afghanistan. And then again when you got to Peshawar. He told me you and Toshi would be with two of his most trusted men. And then I know a few people in Karachi, I asked them to keep their eyes open for you."

I wasn't mad at all; I'd just been feeling strange, probably since Peshawar. Kinda felt like something was up.

"How come Mahmoud called you," I asked him, but I didn't think he'd tell me straight.

"He called me from Sra Kala to tell me that you were ready to head back, and that Toshi was coming with you. Oh and by the way, I've known Toshi for a few years and I made the arrangements for him to meet Mahmoud Shinwari, but I didn't tell you about him because you weren't really working together."

That was about it, Pik was still full of shit.

"All right Jack? See you in a few weeks." he clicked off.

The Chans waited on the boat while Chiang Mai and I went up to get Toshi and The Product, and to settle our account with the mujahids. I'd been gone for a little more than an hour, but they were still waiting for me in the truck.

I introduced Chiang Mai to Jafir, Mazar and Toshi. They exchanged pleasantries, and Chiang Mai asked Mazar to sit in the truck with him so they could go over the business transaction.

I guess Mahmoud told Pik that Mazar was to

be the moneyman, and Pik no doubt told Chiang Mai. Although the truck was parked out of the way, Toshi, Jafir and I stood together with our backs to it, hoping to block any wandering eyes while stuff changed hands.

They finished quickly.

"We should get going by five," said Chiang Mai.

I gave Mazar Pik's number, telling him I could be reached there.

"Call if you need anything," I said, "otherwise I'll see you next season."

I told Jafir I'd see him later too, and shook both their hands. Toshi gave his Galil to Jafir, and the Hardballer to Mazar, then we parted ways.

"Hey Jack, Toksa!" Mazar called after me as we walked down the crowded ramp.

28

Back aboard the boat, I started to introduce Toshi
to the Chans, but they already knew each other.
I shouldn't have been surprised, the Chans body
guarded for Pik whenever he left Hong Kong, and
so they'd probably gone to Tokyo with him whenever he'd meet with Toshi.

I admit that I was slightly nervous about how
the Chans and Toshi would get along, the Chans
being Chinese and Toshi being Japanese; that goes
with Chiang Mai being Thai as well. But there
were no problems.

I also have to admit that I'd wondered, ever
since I saw Toshi kick the shit out of those five in
Peshawar, who was badder; the Chans with their
kung fu, or Toshi with his karate.

The Chans had already prepared a knee-high
mound that covered the floor, wall-to-wall, of the
two meter square by two meter high catch room. The

mound was camouflage: Three thousand kilos of frozen tiger prawns.

When I handed over the two-barrel duffels one at a time, Johnny hooked them to a cable-pulley and hoist mounted to a track in the ceiling, while Joey donned a pair of rubber boots and climbed onto the mound and dug a hole in the center of it with a shovel.

Then Johnny pulled the return line on the pulley, bringing the ninety kilos over the hole; Joey lowered it in and covered it up.

After passing the shovel over to me, the last thing he did before closing the door behind him, was turn off the freezer.

Chiang Mai showed me a cabin full of small arms including six RPG-7s, a couple AKs, and two Browning M-2 .50 caliber machine guns, hand-grenades and plenty of ammunition; tripods for the belt-guns were mounted to the decks–fore and aft.

"In case we see pirates," he said.

At 4:57 p.m. with over eight thousand kilometers to go, we started out of Korangi Harbor into the Arabian Sea.

The first leg would be twenty-four-hundred kilometers south, to the Port of Colombo, Sri Lanka.

"If we can keep our speed constant," Chiang Mai said as we pushed close to twenty knots, "we should make port in a little over fifty hours."

I changed out of my boots, fatigue-pants and long shirt, preferring no shirt, bare feet, and an old pair of baggies I found in a cabin drawer. I saw the three hosed hookah in the closet, and figured the Chans had some buds, but I knew this mission wasn't over yet.

The first night of the voyage, after a great sunset with lots of reds and oranges, Chiang Mai went to sleep early, and the Chans drove.

Toshi and I played chess until two in the morning.

"I never saw your tattoo before," he said, after beating me for the third time in a row, "it is a Kirin is it?"

I nodded, got that tat, on my right shoulder, in Hong Kong, '71. Didn't know anything about it, but at the time it was, and is still to this day, my favorite beer.

He called the top bunk in the remaining cabin, but I just grabbed a blanket, and stretched out on the deck under the stars. I woke as the eastern sky was getting pink, think that means it's going to rain.

It cleared up before noon, and I lounged in a deck chair on the starboard side for the rest of the day and then watched another real nice sunset.

Guess I stuck to the starboard side for almost the whole trip down the West Coast of India. We were probably too far out to see anything on the shore anyway, and besides, I missed the ocean.

A few days of doing nothing but day dreaming on the water was just what I needed. I was staring off into the horizon, thinking about surfing. I don't think Toshi liked the water, he didn't come outside at all; maybe it was his first time on a boat. I remember my first time out to sea with Chiang Mai, I fucking hated it! But now, I was drawn to the ocean as the source of life, it was in my blood.

That night went by uneventfully. I slept on the deck again, until it started raining right before sunrise. By noon, it had turned into a pretty nice day, and I was back on the starboard for most of the afternoon.

Around four o'clock, we started to turn in towards the coast.

"Hey Jack," Chiang Mai called to me from the drive deck, "move over to the port side while we come in closer to the southern tip of India, those mountains are the Western Ghats."

We were still pretty far away, but I could see a few surfers in the water, and it looked like they were getting some pretty decent waves. I wanted to get a few, but would wait for Big Wave Bay. The beaches didn't look all that different from the ones in Hong Kong, white-yellow sand and palm trees. We passed an old lighthouse.

"That's the Kanyakumari Lighthouse," said Chiang Mai, "it's eighty years old, this is Cape Comorin."

"You sound like a tour guide Chiang Mai," I said jokingly, "how do you know so much about India?"

"Neil and I tried a few times, back in the 50s,

to sail from Hong Kong to England, on this same route. We never made it though, usually turned around at the Cape of Good Hope, South Africa."

As the sun dipped closer to the horizon, painting yet another spectacular sunset, we entered the Gulf of Manar.

Soon after, we were eating a big meal Chiang Mai ordered for us: pol sambo, a Maldives fish dish with sweet rice and coconut, and polos pehi, a Jak fruit dish with spicy curry, at a restaurant on the docks in the Sri Lankan capital.

I was surprised to see Toshi eating so much; I figured he'd been puking since we left. The sun had gone down by the time we finished eating, so I didn't get to look around much. After the Chans refueled the boat, we pulled out of Colombo and turned almost 180°, steering southeast into the Bay of Bengal.

The next stop was twenty-two-hundred fifty kilometers away, the Port of Belawan, on the northeast coast of Sumatra.

"Last week when we were coming to Korangi," Chiang Mai was saying, "there was a storm following right behind us, will probably see some of it now. It could get pretty rough, monsoon winds and all."

Only two hours later, the boat was pitching up into the air and then crashing down on the breakers constantly, and it was impossible to see out the windows.

Even on deck I couldn't see anything through

the downpour.

The wind blasted the boat so hard, and it was whistling so loud, I couldn't remember ever seeing a storm like it before. But we kept going, and by the time the sun had climbed halfway to its high point the next day, the sky was blue again and the seas were smooth, and we were through it.

Chiang Mai had planned for storms, so the guns, and especially the ammunition, rockets, grenades–were stored in secure containers; not left to roll around.

Unfortunately, we only made about three-hundred-twenty kilometers that night. So we still had nineteen-hundred kilometers to get another storm or two, but the next forty or so hours were storm free.

The sun had gone down about two hours before, when we pulled in to Belawan; Chiang Mai said we should anchor for the night, and get going in the morning.

"We are at the beginning of a seven-hundred and seventy two-kilometer long corridor between Malaysia and Indonesia known as The Straits of Malacca, it is a hundred-sixty kilometers wide at this end, but it closes to only forty-eight kilometers wide at the other end."

I flashed on the Khyber Pass.

"For centuries pirates have used these Straits as a hunting grounds, channel depths become harder to read as the lane narrows. A favorite tactic is to sink a ship in the center of the channel, thus stopping or slowing traffic, making potential targets easier to attack."

He moved the boat to the right side of the harbor, a short distance away from the docks, and we anchored there.

Before turning in, the Chans set up the M-2s, locked and loaded on fresh boxes, and covered them with tarpaulins. Inside, Toshi set to loading AK magazines with his LULA Mag-Loader.

"This was for the Galil," he said, "but I forgot to give it to Jafir when I gave him the rifle."

I set up three gunner's nests with the sand-filled ballast bags from below deck; one on top of the drive platform and one around each of the Brownings. Each of the nests was complete with two RPGs and two AKs, spare magazines, and extra rocket-grenades were also at the ready.

When the sun came up the next morning, we motored over to the refueling dock.

"If we do take any fire, it's probably better not have too much fuel on board," said Chiang Mai.

Keppel Harbor, Singapore was our next stop, so I only pumped enough to get there.

As we pulled into the center of the channel, heading southeast into the rising sun, there was a light fog ahead, but it was sure to burn off in the next few hours. Other than that, it looked like a perfect day; blue skies, smooth water, and a light breeze across the bow.

A couple steamers and fishing boats trailed us at a comfortable distance, but we were first in line.

Chiang Mai and I were up top, the Chans were doing tai chi on the back deck, and Toshi was working out with them.

"Nice to finally see you out of the cabin," I said to him.

He looked up to see me and smiled.

"Yeah," he said, "I had to get centered, been a while since I was on a boat."

"I figured you were puking."

"No," shaking his head he said, "I don't get motion sick."

At lunchtime I went down to get a few sandwiches and Cokes from the ship's fridge for me, Chiang Mai and Toshi; loaded the chow into a little red neskie and slung it over my shoulder.

Back above, Toshi was standing on the end of the gunwale, with his back to me. I noticed that it seemed to be getting darker.

"I guess that fog hasn't burned off yet, huh?" I said as I approached with his food.

"I don't think it is fog, Jack, smell that?"

I inhaled deeply, catching a whiff of burning leaves and smoldering rubber. I went to the back deck to see if the Chans noticed it too; there I saw that all of the other boats had slowed way down and fallen way behind us.

"Something's going on, keep your eyes open," Chiang Mai called down.

I hurried up the ladder, laid the neskie down next to Chiang Mai, and took up the binocs, looking in front of us first–for anything.

The fog was definitely turning into a rolling black smoke cloud, I couldn't see very far into it. I turned to look behind us; the other boats had turned around and were hauling ass the other way.

Then about nine little Zodiac boats took to the water. Each held four or five guys, and they were racing toward us, about five hundred meters away.

"Toshi, get your RPGs and move to the back, I'll watch the front," Chiang Mai ordered.

I was ready with the RPGs up top, and the Chans were ready off the back; Joey, with an 80-MM mortar, and Johnny, with an M-79.

Chiang Mai was studying the approaching Zodiacs with the binocs.

"Their guns are up, I see mostly AKs and a few old bazookas," he said, "Joey, drop a few mortars on them to check the range."

I'm sure Joey, and Chiang Mai for that matter, knew that mortar fire from a moving boat wouldn't be all that accurate, but sometimes all you need to do is get close.

Joey let off a few, and three big explosions hit about ten feet in front of the lead chasers.

Johnny set the leaf on the thumper to match the mortar's range meter, and blooped off a few grenades. No direct hits were made, but they were all wet and thinking twice about whether or not they wanted to continue the attack.

The others were still coming, and a few more Zodiacs joined the chase, from the back and front. I turned around to face the front.

"Toshi, we need you up front." Chiang Mai called out.

A group of the rubber boats were rushing the bow; less than a hundred meters out. I took aim and fired the RPG-7 at the closest, and then I heard the unmistakable sound of a big helicopter. I closed my eyes, and turned around to see an Mi-24 Hind flying up our six.

This close to home, are you kidding me?!

Over a loudspeaker came a voice speaking an unfamiliar language. It sounded Asian to me; Chiang Mai said it was Malay, and all the Zodiacs immediately broke off their chase and retreated.

The Hind didn't come any closer than about four-hundred meters, and another voice came on, speaking perfect English.

"Mr. Suukho would like to offer his sincere thanks to your employer, Pik Hsun, for the Mi-24. Please stop at the Bahru Marina, just before the Johor-Singapore Causeway, on the Johor Bahru side, to allow him to show his utmost appreciation."

I turned to look at Chiang Mai.

"Pik has been supporting Suukho's Anti-Communist forces since 1968," he said, "the first few marijuana pickups you came along on were from him."

I remembered, so I gave the Hind the thumbs-up.

29

A few hours later, we pulled into the marina. A short thin Asian looking man greeted us at the dock, he spoke in a familiar voice, with an English accent; it was the guy from the Hind loudspeaker.

"I am Goloh," he said, "Mr. Suukho instructed me to invite you all to the Marina Clubhouse for lunch and entertainment, Mr. Suukho apologizes that he is unable, due to prior engagements, to thank you himself."

I hoped he wouldn't be insulted by us rejecting the offer, but explained that we didn't want to get off the boat, I wanted to keep an eye on the H, I didn't tell him that though.

Instead, I welcomed him to come aboard. He did, and had a giant lunch of the local food sent up. He told us what each food was, with a list of the major ingredients, but it was so much that I forget most of it: Kuay Chap—rice soup with pork, doubt, and bean curd, Lor Mee–a noodle dish with a dark soy sauce, fish cake, and bean sprouts, Goreng Pisang–breaded, fried banana slices, Satay–grilled chicken with onions in cucumbers, on skewers, covered in a spicy peanut sauce, Kari Lemak Ayam–chicken curry with coconut milk, and Ikan Bakar–barbecued stingray.

Like I said it was a lot more than that, but those are the ones that stick out. We finished up on a fruit salad made of exotic fruits like: Durian, Mangosteen, Langan, and Rambutan in a light citrus honey syrup. We drank Tiger Beer.

It took so long to eat all that food, and I tried a little bit of everything, that lunch became dinner, and day turned into night.

After the meal, Goloh said he had one more treat for us: five, truly beautiful, Singaporean women who would stay until the next morning.

"I don't mean to refuse such a gift," said Chiang Mai after Goloh left, "but I can't cheat on my wife Jack! Help me out."

So Chiang Mai slept on the bridge that night, Toshi and the Chans each got a woman and a cabin, and I got my own cabin and two women. It had been about nine months since I'd seen any titties, but that night I had four perfect little brown circles to myself.

The next morning, the females left and we got ready to pull out for the twenty-six-hundred kilometers to Kowloon. To make it all the way in a straight run, we of course, would need to refuel

and probably carry a few fifty-gallon drums of pet-
rol on the boat.

"But what if we have to start shooting," Chiang
Mai was still worrying about carrying extra fuel
cans on the boat, "or someone is shooting at us?"

"It's either that, or we have to go into Vietnam,"
I told him–knowing that we couldn't, "we'll just
have to keep watch, and if someone is coming after
us, we can float the fuel drums until they're gone."
The Chans agreed.

We ended up leaving with four fifty-gallon
drums lashed to the deck.

The first four days of the final stretch went by
uneventfully; the ocean was exceptionally calm for
the beginning of June, and lulled by complacency,
we–the Chans and I–smoked the bong, and drank
beers, while Chiang Mai drove the boat.

Toshi wouldn't get high with us, but he at least
came out on deck, sat up on the front of the boat in
the Lotus Position and meditated from sunrise to
sundown everyday.

At night, the Chans would drive the boat, Toshi
would cook a meal for the three of us then go to
the cabin for the night, and I would sit up, talking
to Chiang Mai until he was ready to go to sleep.

The fifth morning, I was peeing off the back of
the boat, and I noticed dark clouds building up behind us.

"The radio reported a big typhoon," said Chiang Mai, "coming from the southwest."

"That's it," I said, "looks like we're going to get

hosed."

A few hours later, the sky was black above us, and giant waves were crashing over the bow; the wind was whipping all around. Everything in the boat that wasn't tied down was rolling around slamming into everything else. Me and the Chans were, again, trying to secure the ordinance, while Toshi was putting all the small furniture–chairs and whatnot into a closet.

"I think if I keep going," Chiang Mai was saying, "we can outrun the worst of it."

So we kept going, but by nightfall it was clear that we weren't going to outrun it.

Then the engine died.

"Either the gas gauge lead has come loose in the tank, which has happened before in stormy seas like this," Chiang Mai said, "or we have just run out of gas."

I remembered the fuel drums tied to the deck, and me and Joey were going to go out and get them, while Johnny went to open the fuel port.

Just as I turned to walk out the door on the left side of the boat, a huge wave, like a wall of water, slammed into the right side of the boat, and it pitched us over so hard I smacked the door jam with my forehead. I was out, but the boat righted itself in the water.

When I woke up on the couch in the map room, I could see sunlight shining in through the window. The sky was blue, and the sea was smooth.

I moved to stand up.

"Easy shooter! Don't get up too fast, you knocked your head real good; you were out for almost six hours.

No reason to get up anyway; the waves washed those fuel drums away, and the dinghy's gone too—so we can't even look for them."

I finally focused, and saw that it was Joey talking to me, he said the others were up top trying to reattach the radio's antenna so we could get a call out, he made me drink some hot tea, then I went to see what Chiang Mai was thinking.

"We are about six-hundred-forty kilometers from Hong Kong Island, close to where Neil took you tanker wave surfing, once we get the radio up we'll call Pík."

Finally, the Chans had the antenna back up and rewired; it had gotten blown down when I got knocked out.

Chiang Mai said I should go back inside and try to get Pik on the line.

"Come in Pik, Triple CJ calling, repeat come in Pik, Triple CJ calling, Hey Pik…this is Jack, come back."

I tried that for about ten minutes, and then Chiang Mai came down and got some needle nose pliers.

"One more adjustment," he said.

I waited a few minutes and tried again.

"Hey Jack!" Pik finally answered. "What's up? Did you see that typhoon they were calling for?"

"Yeah," I said, "long story short, we're out of

gas, Chiang Mai says we're six-hundred-forty kilo-meters away–close to Neil's surfing spot."

Then looking out the window, I saw another boat coming up on us.

"Oh fuck! Chinese Coastal Patrol!" I blurted.

Right away, I started thinking about any guns or other hardware we may have left out.

"Pik, I'll call you back…"

The Chans were thinking the same thing I was, and they both came in to help me make sure there was nothing in plain sight, and that the door to the gun room was closed.

Then we went back out on deck, and the Coastal Patrol boat was tied up alongside us. There was a boarding party looking around, and Chiang Mai was talking to the HMFWIC.

I don't speak Chinese, but I could understand most of what was being said: he was telling the patrol captain that we were prawn fishing off the coast of Singapore, when we heard the news report about the storm coming, so we immediately started back to Kowloon, but the Typhoon got us and we ran out of gas, and our replacement fuel washed away with the dinghy, the storm also broke the radio antenna, but we just fixed it and called Kowloon, they're sending out someone to refuel us, should be about eight hours–not too far off what actually happened…

I think he was buying the story, but he wanted to look in the catch freezer.

"Sure," said Chiang Mai in English, "but the

storm knocked out the freezer's electrical, so I'm sure it's pretty ripe by now."

He stepped to the door, and with noticeable hesitation, pulled on its handle until it opened a crack.

It was a hot still day, and the horrible wreaking stench of three thousand kilos of slowly rotting shrimp quickly filled the air; enclosing the boat in a cloud of fumes that must've tripped his gag reflex.

He quickly pushed the door closed, and while stifling a wretch, not making eye contact with any of us, went back over to his own boat and inside. A few minutes later, his subordinate came over and told Chiang Mai that they would sit with us until our refueling boat came.

I went back in and called Pik.

"I'm sending a seaplane with fifteen hundred liters of diesel," he said, "should be there in a little more than three hours."

Chiang Mai went back out to tell the Coastal Patrol the news. They had untied from the Triple CJ, and anchored just far enough away that they didn't have to smell us. So he bull horned the change of plans over, the Chief's lieutenant gave a gesture of agreement, hooking pinkies, then went back inside.

And just like Pik said, about three and a half hours later the plane arrived.

We refueled and then waved goodbye to the patrol boat.

Eight hours later, we were back in Kowloon—a little more than two weeks after leaving Korangi Harbor.

30

We had been back in Kowloon for a little more than a week. Pik settled up with me; I got $2 million for managing his $5 million deal with the mujahideen.

He told me that he paid Chiang Mai $1 million for transporting the heroin, and the Chans split $1 million for their part. So for ninety kilos of Afghan Brown, he made an initial investment of $10 million total, and would see about $30 million in return.

I borrowed Pik's cabin cruiser, The Dreamer, to get back to all my surfing spots around Hong Kong Island: Big Wave Bay and Shek O, and then on the southeast end: Stanley Bay and Repulse Bay.

Then I took Toshi on a sightseeing tour over to Lantau Island to see the Po Lin Buddhist Monastery on the Ngong Ping Plateau. There were three, a little bigger than life size, bronze statues of the

Buddha representing Past Life, Present Life and Future Life.

There are also a buncha' nice looking mountains over there: Nei Lak Shan, Lin Fa Shan, Sunset Peak and the biggest in Hong Kong, Lantau Peak. But I realized that compared to the Hindu Kush Mountains, the Mountains in Hong Kong are just Hills. On the way back, we saw a school, or is it a pod, of Chinese White Dolphins.

"They're not really white, are they," he asked.

After Lantau and Lamma Islands we went to Uncle Chow's Beach Bar, one of Pik's places, to get some lunch; the daily special was Kirin in a bottle and a grilled American hotdog with cheese.

"How do you think Mazar is doing," asked Toshi.

"I'm sure they're doing fine, Mahmoud and Mazar. He's a pretty smart kid. Oh, you know, I meant to tell you that he's a physics major in college."

"Yeah, he told me…"

A few days later we were eating lunch in Pik's Cafe in Kowloon, and Toshi said he'd made up his mind to go back to Tokyo. He had booked a flight for the following day from Kai Tak Airport. He tried to get me go with him.

"No thanks, I'll be heading back to Afghanistan in a few months, and I think I'm just going to hang out here, drink beer, smoke pot, and surf until then."

"There are a few surfing beaches in Japan," he

said, "one is in Tokushima, Ikumi Beach, I have a small house there, my Mother's childhood home."

"Well, I'll keep that in mind, next time I take a vacation."

Just then, the maitre d' guy came over to tell me I had a phone call, and that Pik said I should take it in his office.

I went through the kitchen doors, and to the right up a flight of stairs. Pik was sitting at his desk with his door open. He didn't say anything as I reached for the waiting phone, but he looked as if there could be a problem.

"Hello, Jack Randall here."

Nothing.

Then, "Hello Jack, this is Mazar...from Peshawar."

I could hear some tension in his voice.

"Hey Mazar! Toshi and I were just talking about you! Everything OK?"

The line was quiet again.

"Mahmoud is dead, so are Jafir, and Khaleed, and a few others from Sra Kala: the Sheik killed them."

His words hit me like a bucket of ice cold water. I immediately looked up at Pik, who was already looking at me with concern.

"There was a spy in Sra Kala after all, it was Hassam, he was the Sheik's spy, and he led us into an ambush in the Pass. The Sheik, a couple of Arabs, and a few Ghilzai Pashtun from Khalq were waiting for us. I'd be dead too if a group of Afridis, friends of my father's, had not happened by."

"Mazar, what can I do?! I can come get you, I'll come to Peshawar, and we'll figure out what to do from there."

"No Jack, the Sheik has taken control of Sra Kala. I only called because you will not be able to do any more business with the mujahideen of the village."

I couldn't tell if he was just talking tough, or if he truly believed that I was only worried about getting more dope.

I was remembering what Mahmoud told me about Pashtunwali, the Pashtun code of honor, and I knew that it would demand that Mazar avenge his father. And that unless he walked away now, he'd be feuding with the Sheik until one of them was dead.

"Come on, Mazar!" I said, "I don't care about doing business there! I'm worried that you'll try to get revenge on that fucker! And that he'll kill you too! Let me come help you…"

I'd never had anyone to give advice to before, but I wanted to try to now.

"Mazar, listen, whenever I talked to Mahmoud about you, he wanted nothing more than a better future for you, for you to reach your potential. He hoped that you would be able to leave Afghanistan-Pakistan someday, come to Hong Kong, bring your Mother. You can go to college, or whatever, and you won't be in the middle of a war anymore."

Hoping I'd said the right stuff, I just waited

for him to start talking.

"I'm sorry Jack; I knew that you were not just mad about being cut off from the opium fields. I said that, because I felt, feel, a little guilty. I feel guilty because I am not going to try to avenge my Father, he grew up with the Pashtunwali, but he got away from it for a while, when he met my Mother in Kabul.

"The war with the Soviets brought him back to that code, that culture. But I have never really known it. I did not want you to think less of me. I did not know, until recently, that he felt that way, about not wanting me to get involved.

"But I think he knew his death was coming, he made arrangements with Mr. Hsun to set up an international bank account for me and my mother. Mr. Hsun deposited $1 million into it–for the Hind that you and Toshi took from the Soviets."

I was startled, and when I looked at Pik I'm sure he could tell.

"And he also gave me a phone number to get in touch with his sister, Barik, I never even knew he had a sister. She lives in San Francisco, California. My Mother and I are going to America, leaving tomorrow. You should come see us some time."

He was quiet for a minute.

"Toksa, Jack…"

It took me a minute, but suddenly I knew what I was going to do.

"Yeah, Yeah, when you get there, send me your address, Toksa, Mazar."

I hung up the phone, and looked back at Pik.
"Everything OK?"

"Well, Mahmoud is dead," I said as I walked to the door, "but his son, Mazar, got the money you sent him."

I left the office to head back down stairs to talk some more about Tokushima.

"Hey Pik," I stopped, remembering that he had taught me how to surf. I turned and said, "You know, for a gangster-drug dealer, you're a pretty good guy."

I started with a straight face, and ended up smiling. Pik was smiling too.

"I think I'm going to take a few months vacation to go to Japan with Toshi," I paused then added, "and then maybe San Francisco."

About the Author

Ben Dowling was born in St. Petersburg in 1971. He went to Dixie Hollins High School, graduating in 1989. He started taking classes at St. Petersburg Junior College (now St. Petersburg College), and later transferred to the University of South Dakota in Vermillion where he received two Bachelors Degrees, English 1996, Physics & Mathematics (double major) 2002, and a Masters Degree in Mathematics 2004.

Dowling was diagnosed with Friedrichs ataxia when he was 11 years old, and after living independently for 17 years, was forced to return to Florida. He now lives with his parents in St. Petersburg.

He writes with Dragon NaturallySpeaking voice recognition software.

The inspiration for the Soviet-Afghan war story came from his teenage years spent reading *Soldier of Fortune* magazine and from America's more recent involvement in the country.